Praise for th

"The irrepressible hero. ～～～ ～～～ ～～ ongoing banter is nonstop fun."

— *Ellery Queen Mystery Magazine*

"Lynn captures the flavor of the South, right down to the delightfully quirky characters in this clever new mystery series. Elli Lisbon is the Stephanie Plum of the South!"

— Krista Davis,
New York Times Bestselling Author of the Domestic Diva Mysteries

"Elli Lisbon is proving herself to be the most lovable OCD PI since Adrian Monk."

— Maddy Hunter,
Agatha-Nominated Author of the Passport to Peril Series

"A must-read mystery with a sassy sleuth, a Wonderland of quirky characters, and a fabulous island setting that will keep you turning pages."

— Riley Adams,
Author of the Memphis Barbecue Mysteries

"Back for another episode of juggling sleuthing, professional responsibilities, and complicated personal relationships...Lynn whips all these ingredients into a tasty southern mash of star-crossed romance, catty but genteel one-upsmanship, and loveable oddballs that should please fans of humorous cozies."

— *Alfred Hitchcock Mystery Magazine*

"A solid and satisfying mystery, yes indeed, and the fabulous and funny Elliott Lisbon is a true gem! Engaging, clever and genuinely delightful."

— Hank Phillippi Ryan,
Agatha, Anthony and Macavity Award-Winning Author

"With an intelligent woman sleuth, a unique blend of quirky supporting characters and a well-devised mystery plot, *Board Stiff* is delightfully entertaining."
— *Fresh Fiction*

"A sparkling new voice in traditional mystery."
— CJ Lyons,
New York Times Bestselling Author

"Elli is an admirable and engaging heroine. Deft writing and clever dialogue further ensure that readers will be looking forward to the next installment in Elli's adventures."
— *Kings River Life Magazine*

"An engaging read that grabbed my attention from the start...With witty banter, a likable cast of characters and a visually appealing setting, this is a great start to what I hope is a long running series."
— *The Cozy Chicks*

"'I used to be able to juggle six wet cats while balancing a bowl of Jell-O on my head. Now I couldn't locate a cat if I stood in a barn with a can of tuna in one hand and a mouse in the other.' Elliott's self-effacement makes her an unusually lovable protagonist, especially when she lets fly with comments like that."
— *Mystery Scene Magazine*

"I loved this book! The location, off the Atlantic coast and typically warm, and the quirky characters that keep showing up really help to make this a delightful and entertaining read."
— *BookLikes*

"Packed with humor, romance, danger and adventure, this is a good mystery full of plot twists and turns, with red herrings a plenty and an ending that I found both surprising and satisfying."
— *Cozy Mystery Book Reviews*

POT LUCK

The Elliott Lisbon Mystery Series
by Kendel Lynn

Novels

BOARD STIFF (#1)
WHACK JOB (#2)
SWAN DIVE (#3)
POT LUCK (#4)

Novellas

SWITCH BACK
(in OTHER PEOPLE'S BAGGAGE)

AN ELLIOTT LISBON MYSTERY

POT LUCK

Kendel Lynn

HENERY PRESS

POT LUCK
An Elliott Lisbon Mystery
Part of the Henery Press Mystery Collection

First Edition
Trade paperback edition | December 2016

Henery Press
www.henerypress.com

All rights reserved. No part of this book may be used or reproduced in any manner whatsoever, including Internet usage, without written permission from Henery Press, except in the case of brief quotations embodied in critical articles and reviews.

Copyright © 2016 by Kendel Lynn
Cover art by Natalie Hutcherson

This is a work of fiction. Any references to historical events, real people, or real locales are used fictitiously. Other names, characters, places, and incidents are the product of the author's imagination, and any resemblance to actual events or locales or persons, living or dead, is entirely coincidental.

Trade Paperback ISBN-13: 978-1-63511-125-5
Digital epub ISBN-13: 978-1-63511-126-2
Kindle ISBN-13: 978-1-63511-127-9
Hardcover Paperback ISBN-13: 978-1-63511-128-6

Printed in the United States of America

For Charlie

ACKNOWLEDGMENTS

I'm blessed with encouragement and love and support from so many around me, I'm forever thankful.

Thank you to Pat Allen Werths, Ellie Enos, Femmes Fatales, Sisters in Crime, Lane Buckman, Dru Ann Love, and much love to my mom, Suzanne Atkins.

There aren't enough hugs in the land to express my gratitude for the authors and staff of Henery Press. An extra bucket of appreciation to Erin George, Rachel Jackson, and Amber Parker. Please know I will always be grateful.

Thank you to Art Molinares for letting the dream fly, and to Diane Vallere, a once-in-a-lifetime friend.

ONE

(Day #1: Saturday Morning)

I walked the dirt path from the parking lot to the main road of Fisher's Landing Trailer Park and Yacht Club, counting two spots until I reached number three. I'd barely placed one sneaker on the plastic grass when two brown dogs barreled toward me. Barking and snapping with their legs rushing at full speed. I was nearly trampled to death. Seeing how they were no larger than a pair of Beanie Babies, I survived.

Whilst I rolled around in love at first sight, and not kidding, in my complete time on Planet Earth, I'd never seen something as cute as those pug puppies, with their silky tan coats and squishy black faces, Lola Carmichael exited her Airstream with a snap of her gum and a swing of her hip. Both trailer and owner were circa 1952—*Mad Men* had nothing on Lola Carmichael. She wore her beehive like a helmet and kept her jewelry plastic. Today it was all glittered and green.

"Aren't they marvelous?" Lola tossed down what look like two petrified Slim Jims and the pugs abandoned me. They settled on the ten foot patch of AstroTurf that covered her front lawn area, gnawing on their mini logs. "That's Colonel Mustard and Mrs. White. My new watch dogs. Though someone could steal my whole kit and caboodle and those two wouldn't notice with a Bully Stick in front of 'em. Don'tcha just want to scoop them up and put 'em in your pocket?"

"Immediately." And I meant it. Metaphorically. I like my pets the same way I like my children. Under someone else's ownership.

Lola dusted off an aluminum chair, the kind with frayed vinyl slats, and gestured for me to sit. "Thanks for popping over, Elli. I know you're busy with the big party today and all, but when I saw you park at Tug's, I saw it as fate. I could really use your help. A favor, really."

"Of course," I said.

Lola fidgeted. First with her hair. Then her nails. Then the turquoise princess phone sitting on the table. Its twenty-foot cord wound across the lawn patch and through the screen door of the trailer. "Can I getcha some pretzel salad? Made a fresh batch this morning."

"Pretzel salad? That's a thing?"

"Sure is. Jell-O, fresh pineapple, gooseberries. Irish cream, homemade. And not to brag, but mine's kind of legend here in the park. It's the Pennsylvania pretzel base. Makes it slap-your-grandma-in-the-face good."

"Huh. Well, I ate an enormous breakfast, but maybe next time." Or never. Jell-O, pretzels, and Irish cream?

"How about a lemonade? With iced tea? Or just iced tea? I've got instant coffee, put a dollop of Irish cream in there?" Lola jumped up so fast, she startled Colonel Mustard. He barked and yipped until she rubbed behind his velvet puppy ears in reassurance that all was safe.

"Lola, what can I help you with?" I asked, discreetly shifting my bottom into a more comfortable section of the pre-worn chair slats.

"I know I'm not one of your fancy donors," Lola said, easing back into her chair, crossing her legs, adjusting her top. "But I always give to the Children's Hospital Wonderland Tea."

"We appreciate your support. Whatever you need, Lola." As Director of the billion-dollar Ballantyne Foundation, I often helped many an islander with discreet inquiries. It was part of my job description. And I was in hot pursuit of my PI license to help my endeavors. Only four thousand hours until I was official.

"Vivi Ballantyne helped me out of a jam. Really more than one, honest to Pete. She's always been good to me, you know?"

"Absolutely. Vivi adores you. I'll help in any way I can."

"Which probably means I owe her, not the other way around," Lola said. "I get that. But I need the help."

"Lola, I'll help," I said, trying to sound patient as Lola dragged her feet as if she was about to ask me for a kidney.

"Vivi is the one person I trust with my life, certainly with my business." Lola waved her arms in the vicinity of the trailer park. "And if she trusts you with her Ballantyne—"

I reached out to touch her shoulder and nearly toppled over in the lightweight nine-ounce aluminum chair. I righted myself. "Lola, I'm in."

She scooched in closer, the chair softly rattling against the plastic grass. "Someone paid off my mortgage. Here at Fisher's Landing."

"For your trailer?"

"For the park," she said. "Like I said, my whole kit and caboodle."

"Someone paid your mortgage, and this is bad?"

"My luck ain't that good." She walked over to the screen door and popped inside.

I knew she was the manager, had been as long as I'd lived on Sea Pine Island, but owner?

She came out and handed me a folder. "Here's everything on the place. Fisher's Landing. I got the trailer park and yacht club in my divorce settlement. Tug owns Tug's, but I lease him the land. Standard lease. He pays on time. I've always had a mortgage on the Landing. But lately I've been running behind on payments. Like for a few months. Maybe more than a few. Close to six. I was headed to the lawyer's today to look at bankruptcy options."

I leaned in, one hand on her arm, the other on the folder. "Oh, Lola, things are that bad?"

"Well, not anymore. And that worries me."

I glanced through the folder. Looked like standard paperwork not meant to be understood at a glance. More like a two-hour sit down with a dictionary, a thesaurus, and a doctorate degree in financial management. "I'll look into it first thing Monday, see what I can find out."

Lola actually smiled for the first time since I arrived. "You're the best, Elliott."

I hoisted myself from the clingy chair slats, folder in one hand. I casually rubbed Colonel Mustard's belly with the other until he yipped at me. Probably thought I was going to swipe his Bully Stick and run. "You coming to the Irish Spring at the Big House?"

"I thought that's usually a nighttime shindig," Lola said.

"We switched it this year. A beer tasting and corned beef cabbage cook-off is better held on the back lawn in the sunshine." The Ballantyne held the largest St. Patrick's Day party on the island. Half fundraiser, half excuse to host a backyard party. "You should come, Lola."

"No, not me. Those foodies and I go way back." She fluffed her hair hat. "Really way back. Not my crowd."

"It'll be fun. I know you love St. Patrick's Day." I gestured to her tight green top, sparkly green nails, and dangling clover earrings. It was a lot of green, considering the official holiday was still three days away.

She smiled and touched her earrings. "I can't. I had a falling out with the chefs."

"All of them? The cook-off features about twenty different chefs."

Lola shrugged. "Most. The Carmichael clan, anyhoo."

Chef Carmichael, who owned a renowned eatery on Sea Pine Island, had participated in many a Ballantyne function. He'd never served on our board, but we still considered him one of our own.

Lola Carmichael, Chef Carmichael. I'd never put it together. "You're related to Chef?

"By divorce. My ex is his brother. I kept the trailer and the park, he kept his girlfriend and the Winnebago. They drive-in for the Savannah St. Pat's parade every year."

"Carmichael is Scottish, though, right?"

"Yes, but green beer is still beer."

"They won't be at the Ballantyne party. Chef Carmichael, yes, but the rest of the clan, no. I've never met them nor seen a Winnebago in valet." With a last pat to Mrs. White, ignoring the temptation to actually stick her in my pocket and abscond, I walked toward the drive. "Think about it, Lola. Vivi would be delighted if you came to the Irish Spring."

"You'll call me on Monday when you find out?" Lola asked with a nod to the folder.

I held it up. "Definitely. Who knows? Maybe you have a secret admirer."

She swung her hip. "My admirers don't keep me a secret."

I laughed and headed toward Tug Jensen standing near my Mini convertible. I had wedged it into a half-spot reserved for scooters near the entertainment center slash laundry room of the trailer park.

"I saw you head to Lola's after you pulled up," Tug said. He was a scruffy man who looked like he owned a bar in a trailer park, one appropriately named Tug Boat Slim's. "Everything okay?"

"Everything's great," I said. "Sorry I'm a little late."

"Perfect timing, actually," he said. He held an eight-foot Blue Marlin, complete with a two-foot, razor-sharp spear nose. Spear bill? Upper-jaw portion of its face. I was never sure if Tug had caught this sucker in the wild or if he'd purchased it off eBay, but when he handed it to me and I didn't tip over from its weight, I had my answer. "Thanks for the help," Tug said. "We're all packed up, but Marley needs special handling. He's the centerpiece of our display. You got this?"

I glanced from the eight-foot fish to my three-foot backseat. "Sure, Tug. See you there."

He trotted off to a line of trucks stuffed with grills and pots and chowder-making goods, all headed to the Big House. Another of my directorship duties: making sure the Irish Spring ran smoothly. Even if that included barreling down Cabana Boulevard with a fiberglass marlin precariously perched out the back of my Mini Coop.

I stood it upright in the backseat (not on the leather, I'm not a hillbilly) with its tail resting comfortably on the floor and its spear pointing jauntily toward the sky. With Marley secure (ish), I snapped my seatbelt and drove out of the mostly empty lot. Only two cars left behind. One I didn't recognize and one I did. Bitsy Obermeyer's. Her Mercedes stuck out like a Pucci kaftan at a yard sale. Also because it was pink. I glanced around but didn't see her, and Tug's bar looked empty.

I didn't give it another thought, and with nary a care, I zipped down Cabana Boulevard away from the Palmetto Bridge that connected the island to South Carolina. The sun was bright and the briny air whipped around me, the luck of the Irish breezing me along toward the Ballantyne's Big House and the Irish Spring backyard party.

I'd never been great at recognizing the foreshadows life offered me. I once had a platter of petit fours slung at me and I never saw it coming. But like my dear friend Mary Poppins once mused, something was brewing and whatever was to happen had happened before. Or maybe it was Burt who predicted the change in the winds. Either way, that weather vane flipped directions, and me and my merry marlin didn't even notice. That damn stupid ridiculous oversized fiberglass juggernaut shoved into my backseat. It changed my life. And not for the better.

TWO

(Day #1: Saturday Afternoon)

The Ballantyne Big House manse served as the headquarters for the Ballantyne Foundation as well as home to Edward and Vivi Ballantyne. It earned its nickname the old-fashioned way: it looked like a Big House. Also, the number of peccadillos, transgressions, and misdemeanors may have been more suited to an episode of *Orange is the New Black*—if it were G-rated and performed by an all American cast of *Downton Abbey*. The Big House had grandeur and grace and sat up high surrounded by acres of magnolias and live oaks, sharing its splendor with all of Oyster Cove Plantation. At least what one could see from the front.

Today the front looked elegant and bright. Flowers blooming in oversized pots bordered the long drive. The last of the lumbering delivery trucks drove away, while the gardening staff finished draping the front banisters with green, white, and orange silks. We'd been planning the party for a month, actively setting up for three days. While most folks enjoyed parties that raged late into the night, I preferred our leisurely afternoon garden parties. Especially those that included table after table of chef-driven Crock-Pot cookery.

After I handed the marlin to one of Tug's servers and juggled three chefs needing immediate attention, I carried eighteen platters of Guinness chocolate cake cups in four trips. With everything running mostly on time, I went into my office to change. Normally I'd just drive the two miles down to my cottage, but time was tight and I needed every minute I could save. I stared at two garment bags, trying to talk myself out of wearing the same outfit I wore last year. And the year before. Possibly one other year. I only had so many green garments (two) and this particular dress looked really great on me. Good on me. Decent. That's my bar.

"Elliott!" Tod Hayes, Ballantyne Administrator, hollered for me. From directly outside my door. "Guests are arriving. Slap on your good flip-flops and get out here."

I grabbed the familiar Monique Lhuillier sleeveless fit and flare that was more French chartreuse than Kelly green and figured I'd call it my lucky outfit. Like a uniform. It worked for Michael Kors. The man wore the same outfit every day. Certainly I can sport a lucky outfit at a St. Patrick's Day party four years in a row.

The Ballantyne property spanned seventy-five acres. It included courts for croquet, tennis, badminton, plus gardens for vegetables, roses, and meditation. Once out the patio doors, I walked past the sparkling pool lined with chaises adorned with turquoise and lime pillows to the stretch of lawn where the area's top chefs had set up gourmet cook-off stations. Each furnished with island décor from their restaurants. Chefs from Savannah, Charleston, and here on Sea Pine Island competed in the annual Pot of Gold Cook-Off with a seriousness reserved for national competitions, as if this particular competition got them one step closer to a James Beard Award. Considering our prize was a ten-inch tall gold clover trophy, perhaps ours might be better.

Sweet tangy scents from twenty batches of corned beef swirled around the chefs and their staff members. I perused the usual cook-off fare: whiskey-glazed corned beef and cabbage, braised corned beef flat-cut brisket, and my favorite: corned beef spring rolls with a Russian dressing dipping sauce.

Nick Ransom, full-time lieutenant, part-time boyfriend, and one-time love of my life, came up behind me and kissed my neck. My skin tingled and traces of his woodsy cologne blended in contrast to the sea-salted air. "You look lovely," he said.

"Thank you," I said and twirled to face him. "It's my lucky dress."

"Lucky, huh?" He leaned in close, his lips two inches from mine.

"You feeling lucky?" I asked.

"As a matter of fact, I am." He kissed me. Warm and gentle, then deeper, as if the house were on fire and we were lucky to escape the flames.

"Well, not here, Lieutenant Lucky," I said, pulling back and looking up at him. Light lines now fanned out from his eyes, his black hair speckled with dark gray. We'd met in college some twenty something years earlier and would've stayed in love forever had he not disappeared one night leaving me with a broken heart and a determination to never experience that again.

Until he waltzed back in last year. My determination waned from time to time.

"I have a party to host," I said.

I smoothed my dress and he grabbed my hand.

"Let's get away," he said.

"Today? I'm kind of busy."

"Ha. How about this weekend? You, me, a bottle of wine. We'll fly to Fiji."

"And trade one island for another?"

"Yes, but one where we know no one." He kissed my lips, lingering softly for a full two seconds, then walked toward the long line of cook-off stations.

Ah, I thought, as I spotted Matty Gannon in the mingling crowd behind me. I waved to him, he waved back.

Matty was Headmaster at Sea Pine Prep and also one of my best friends. One I dated for a short time. And then stopped when Ransom came back into town and into my life, and boy, did that change everything. Though I'm not sure Matty and I should've been more than friends. He liked to kayak and hike and sail and I liked to not do those things. He wanted kids and a big family and wanted me to not be in love with Nick Ransom. The man who now spent more time at the Big House than most board members ever since Matty became one of those board members. Not possessive, not jealous. Just there more.

Carla Otto, Ballantyne head chef and all-round mother hen, approached as I restrained myself from sneaking a spring roll from the nearest table. "Everyone's checked in and set up and only four complaints. Five if you count Chef Carmichael, and we both know he does not count."

Chef Carmichael owned The Wharf, one of the finest dining establishments on the island. He also had a fierce rivalry with our Carla. Though Carla was winning. Chef just didn't know it.

"Anything else?"

"Nope. Zibby's set to ring the bell in—" Carla checked her watch. "Four minutes." She nodded toward the platter of corned beef spring rolls. "Already secured you two. Plus, I made your favorite Reuben. It's in the kitchen."

"With coleslaw and Russian dressing? The way Edward X. Delaney makes it?"

"The way I make it. With love and soul, and sister, this may be my best one yet. With a side of bread pudding with whiskey sauce."

"Thank you, Carla," I said with a mild swoon. "You're irreplaceable."

"Don't I know it."

"Let me tell you what I know," said a voice that made my skin itch.

"Oh boy," Carla said and made her escape.

"Tate Keating," I said. "How nice of you to cover the Irish Spring. The Pot of Gold Cook-Off is one of our most popular events."

His jolly newsboy cap sat askew on his head, giving him the appearance of a dashing 1920s reporter rather than the tabloid headline-hunting modern-day hound he was.

"Would not miss it for all the green beer in Savannah. The Ballantyne always gives me my best headlines."

The opening bell rang in the distance. The Ballantyne Irish Spring had sprung. I tugged Tate's sleeve, then looped my arm through his, pretending to stroll across the lawn toward the Big House and away from the festivities. We passed streams of patrons dressed in shades of green from emerald to mint as the folk band began to play. I wasn't sure they were Irish. I only know Bono and Enya, and let me tell you, they were no Enya.

"*Ballantyne Ballerina Takes Swan Dive* was neither your best headline nor was it even accurate," I said, referring to a scandal that had taken place last December. "She wasn't a Ballantyne Ballerina."

"It was a Ballantyne production. Means the same thing to me and the *Islander Post* readers." He tried to unhook my arm from his, but I locked on tight and kept pulling him on a path away from the partygoers.

"It's not the same thing," I said as we rounded the hedge corner toward the Zen garden entrance. "The Ballantyne sponsored the *Nutcracker Suite*, that's it. The dancers did not work for us."

"Tomato, tomahto."

"Look, Tate, today's celebration is a longstanding tradition. We kick off spring here on the island." I looked at him with my most sincere imploringest intense gaze. "I kindly request you write about the optimistic, upbeat, cheerful vibe here at the Big House. Keep your headline happy."

Tate stopped moving as if a switch had flipped to off, and I got yanked back. I looked in front of me instead of up at him.

Lola Carmichael lay flat on the grass. Unmoving. Blood slowly seeped from a wound in her chest. Made by a large knife. Held by Chef Carmichael.

"Holy Jesus," I whispered.

"The luck of the Ballantyne," Tate mumbled. "It's all bad luck."

"Call 911," Chef shouted. "Hurry, Elliott. Please hurry."

I fumbled for my phone, fell to my knees, grasped Lola's hand, all at once.

"I'm dialing," Tate said.

I choked, then turned. "Call 911, Tate, not your office." I waved him off and focused on Lola. "No, no, no. Chef, please no." Lola's glittery green nails sparkled in my hand as a slow stream of blood rolled down her arm. I texted Ransom and Sid, in that order, with one hand, the same message: Emergency. Zen garden. Hurry.

Chef Carmichael kept pressure on the area around the knife, his hands sticky red. "I'm so sorry, Lola, I'm so sorry." Chef repeated his remorse over and over. Half whisper, half mumble. Half sob, half disbelief.

Sirens wailed in the distance, rushing closer. People crowded into the hedge opening of the garden. I felt the press of their stares, their gasps, their horror behind me.

Zibby Archibald pushed her way to the front. She was our oldest board member. Eighty-seven, rotund, slightly daffy, completely adorable. She wore a glittered top hat on her recently green-dyed old-lady hairdo. We locked eyes and she gave me a slight nod. "Now, now, everyone, let's leave Miss Carmichael in peace," she said, herding patrons and donors away from the garden entrance. "She needs our discretion. Shall we wrap up the pots of gold? It'll give us something to do."

No matter how many spots I checked on Lola's wrist, a pulse never beat. I watched Zibby go, my chin on my shoulder, tears on my face. She looked back at me with another nod. One that conveyed a thousand sorrows.

THREE

(Day #1: Saturday Afternoon)

Nick Ransom, who I'm sure no longer considered my green dress lucky, tried to console me. He just didn't know how.

"Do you need some water?" He tried to hand me a perky green paper cup.

We gathered in my office. Me and Sid on the sofa, Ransom halfway between me and the door.

"I can't breathe," I said through hiccupping sobs. "This can't be happening. I don't. It wasn't. She's here."

"Harry will take care of her," Ransom said.

"No! Don't say that." I buried my face in my hands. I could not think about the medical examiner caring for Lola Carmichael. His gurney. His zippered bag. His cold and steel room. It wasn't right.

"Oh, sweetie." Sid Bassi, my dearest closest friend of all friends, wrapped me in a hug.

I clung to her, clutching her silky top in my fists. "Don't leave me," I whispered. Gushing tears soaked her blouse.

"I'm here," she said softly. She slipped me a pocket-size hand-sani.

"It's my fault," I said through throaty tears. "I told Lola to come. I told her Vivi would want her here at the party. I saw her this morning. She was bright and vivacious and lively and normal, and oh, Sid, what about Colonel Mustard and Mrs. White?"

"Colonel who?" Ransom asked.

I felt Sid shake her head at Ransom in a "not now" gesture.

"Sid, what did I do?" I sat up. Clicked the sani lid open and closed, open and closed, periodically dousing my hands, rubbing them, then back to opening and closing the lid. It grounded me. "How did this happen? Did I do this? I did this."

"You didn't do this, I swear." Sid rubbed my back and held my hand. "This is not your fault."

"We have Chef Carmichael in custody, Elli," Ransom said.

"You what?" Jane Walcott Hatting marched into the room wearing a chic jade chemise and a scowl to end all scowls. She was a stalwart of prominent Savannah society and chair of the Ballantyne Board. "How dare you arrest Chef Carmichael on the Ballantyne grounds! What a simpleton. Just because Chef found Lola, it means nothing."

"Yes, he was with Lola—"

"Found Lola," Jane said. "He found her, not was with her."

"He was also clutching a knife over her body covered in blood," Ransom said.

"He said it wasn't what it looked like." Jane pointed her finger at Ransom's face. "I heard him tell you. Don't you deny it."

"Jane, I understand you're distressed. I assure you the Sea Pine Police will—"

"You're denying it? He is absolutely incapable of murder and you're going to railroad him like you've done before."

"I've never railroaded anyone, including Chef Carmichael," Ransom said.

"You railroaded me," Jane shouted. "And now this. Chef. This can't be happening."

Ransom looked at me, my earlier words now repeated by Jane. We'd had tragedy and turmoil within our Ballantyne ranks, but this one hit close to home. It was in our home. Ransom's resigned look conveyed exactly what I was thinking. This would not be easy, even if it looked easy.

Corporal Lillie Parker spoke from the doorway. She was as fluid as a ballet dancer and the tallest person in the room. I considered her my friend on the force. "Almost done with the interviews, Lieutenant." She turned to Jane, who glared, so she then turned to me, softening her voice. "Do you have a security detail here at the Big House?"

I wiped my face with shaky hands. "Not a detail. We have a security system and enough staff to run Buckingham Palace, but not a formal security team. We never needed one." Until today. We'd had crime on the island, even murder. It wasn't as rare as one might assume. But this was different. This was the Big House. It was supposed to be untouchable.

"Where are the security cameras? Back lawn, front drive, that kind of thing?" Parker asked.

"No cameras. Edward didn't think we needed them. Neither did I. Why would we need cameras at the Ballantyne? There are motion detectors throughout the house, especially in the upper floors. You know, in the Ballantyne residence." My voice cracked at the word residence. Vivi Ballantyne. How could I tell her? Thank the good Lord in Heaven Vivi and Edward, the generous founders of the Foundation who had treated me like a daughter since I met them some thirty-five years earlier, were traveling in Greenland.

Parker jotted in a notebook, then looked at Ransom. "Valet is almost clear, one vehicle to go. We're looking for the owner of the Winnebago."

"Winnebago?!" Jane and I said at the same time.

I glanced at Jane, then Parker. "Here? In valet?"

Zibby Archibald peeked around Parker. "That's Jessie Carmichael's. He brings it down every year."

"Down from where?" Jane asked.

"You know Jessie?" I asked.

"Sure," Zibby said. "Lola's ex-husband. And their daughter Lucy."

I doubled over and put my head between my knees. Lucy Carmichael. I forgot the existence of Lucy Carmichael. I'm a horrible person. "Parker, please make sure someone cares for Lola's puppies," I choked out, my head still firmly wedged downward. "Colonel Mustard and Mrs. White."

"I'll get a neighbor on it."

"Zibby, why don't we look for this Jessie Carmichael," Ransom said. "I'd like to look at that Winnebago."

"Damned right we're going to look at that Winnebago," Jane said.

I heard them leave. Footsteps and random words faded in the distance. Quiet settled over the room. I could still barely breathe.

"You knew Lucy Carmichael, too?" Sid asked softly. "I barely remember her."

"Lucy and I were close one summer," came my muffled reply. "The summer I moved here after college. Maybe the summer after. I guess that's, what? Nearly twenty years ago?" I sat up, gulped in the cool air of my office. Someone had opened the windows. A light breeze brought in the salty scents of the sea. "Lucy was in the eighth grade, heading to high school. Lola was worried she was mixing with the wrong crowd. She asked Vivi for help. Vivi thought I'd make a good mentor. Really, I think Vivi knew we both needed a friend."

I got up and grabbed a tissue from the top of my desk. Blew my nose and tossed it in the trash. I clutched another tissue before returning to the sofa next to Sid. "Lucy helped me decorate my cottage. I'd just inherited it. We went to the beach and read mysteries and played board games well past bedtime. I worked at the Ballantyne and Lucy helped me get settled. She even helped me with my first case: The Case of the Missing Golf Cart, we called it." A small smile snuck up. "It was interesting and fun and Lucy was a sharp detective. The next Veronica Mars. It was probably three years before my next case and a good ten years before I decided to pursue an honest PI license, but it was my first experience fresh out of being a criminology major and Lucy was clever. As clever as Lola is sassy. Was sassy."

I looked at Sid, shame breaking my heart. "I didn't even mention Lucy to Lola yesterday. I didn't ask about her or how she was doing or where she was living. I'm literally the worst person."

Tod Hayes, my right-hand man at the Ballantyne, came in. He looked both tired and panicked, a contradiction to his perfectly ordered appearance: tidy hair, trim suit, sharp shoes. "We're wrapped up. All the guests have departed." He winced. "Gone home. The staff is cleaning up the mess." He winced again. "What they can, anyway."

I nodded longer than I should have, and he gave a slight nod back, then walked away. I wanted to sit on that sofa forever. I wanted to pretend the day never happened. That I was safe in my cottage and never went to Fisher's Landing Trailer Park and Yacht Club to pick up a stupid plastic fish. No fish pickup, ergo, no meeting with Lola. It would've waited until Monday.

Sid squeezed my hand, bringing me back to reality.

"I need to make sure everything is, well, I don't know, but I need to make sure." I hugged her, clinging more than hugging, and said goodbye. I then spent ten minutes in the restroom. First crying, then splashing cool water over my face and arms.

I walked across the foyer and found Jane standing on the

front steps, barking at someone from Carla's kitchen staff. "I do not care. I cannot even deal with you right now."

She spun around and nearly knocked me down. "That so-called lieutenant of yours arrested the wrong man. But I guess that shouldn't surprise me. He has a system: arrest first and find the truth later. How can you stand it?"

"I—"

"Rhetorical, Elliott. We both know you stand it and he does what he wants." She stormed two steps across the marble floor, her heels clacking with every march, swung the heavy front door, and slammed it in my face.

The medical examiner's van peeked out from the porte cochere. I slowly descended the wide steps as Dr. Harry Fleet wrote on a clipboard. Two men in uniforms loaded a gurney into the back. Three crime scene techs walked down the sidewalk toward the back gate, heavy cases in each hand.

"You'll perform the autopsy, Harry?" I asked.

He looked as if he was about to gruff out his normal brusque response, but the evidence of my distress must have stopped him.

He nodded. "This afternoon, if I can. Tomorrow morning at the latest."

"Thank you," I said and walked back along the pavers toward the front steps.

Tate Keating's MG Roadster was parked caddywhompus at the end of the drive. He peeked out of the convertible top and snapped several photos. The medical examiner's van against the Big House backdrop. He caught my eye, shrugged, then sped away.

It was another hour before I drove down the winding road from the Big House to my cottage. It fronted the Atlantic and never had the soothing tide sounded so lonely. My phone rang within minutes of me walking through the door.

"Hi," Ransom said.

"Hi."

"Is Sid with you?"

"She went home."

"That a good idea?"

"I thought it was at the time."

"You going to be okay tonight?"

I knew what he meant. He was at the station. With Chef Carmichael. The man who killed Lola Carmichael. Or at least the man he thought killed Lola Carmichael.

"You know I'm here if you need me, right, Red?"

"I know. I'll call if I need you."

Ransom and I talked a few more minutes. Extra nice, extra care. I think we both knew this might be the last nice conversation we'd have for a while. We both knew Ransom did not want me involved in this case, but we both knew I was going to get involved anyway.

FOUR

(Day #2: Sunday Morning)

Morning took forever to arrive. I stared at the skylight above my bed, as I had been since I crawled beneath the worn handmade quilt the night before. First I watched the pale evening light fade to midnight black. Then watched as brilliant white flecks speckled the sky. Finally watching the sparkly spots dim as the sun slowly crested somewhere, lightening the inky background to smoky gray to pale blue.

Sundays were as close to a day off as I got. Sleep in, lounge around. Maybe get dressed in grown up clothes. Typically, I sat on the patio and read. Or I put the top down on the Mini and raced around the island, letting the wind lead me on a trip to nowhere. But not on this Sunday. Today's trip had a dreadful destination: the morgue.

I showered and dressed in twenty minutes—I have a routine that hasn't changed since I was old enough to shampoo my own hair—and climbed into the Mini at nine a.m. on the nose. I backed out of my driveway and nearly right into Ransom. He stood on the edge of the curb holding two lidded paper cups.

"Good morning, Red," he said and held out a cup.

"Morning, Ransom." I got out and leaned against the door of the Mini Coop. "You're here early."

Ransom was dressed in wealthy businessman attire: a smooth tailored suit and understated silk tie. Not how one would picture a well-seasoned island lieutenant. Except this former FBI sharpshooter had cleverly chosen his stock purchases, giving him the ability to retire to Sea Pine with a bazillion dollars and the lieutenant's position.

He shook the cup in his outstretched hand so I could hear the ice rattle. I took the proffered beverage and gulped down the fizzy Pepsi. I like my morning caffeine freezing cold and filled with sugar.

"You running errands?" Ransom asked. "Getting a jump on the day?"

"You know very well I'm headed to visit Harry."

"I thought perhaps that's where you were going. But I'm saving you a trip. The knife to the chest said it all. Homicide."

"Yes, I caught that. So nothing new?"

"Nothing new."

"Something you're not telling me?"

"Not on this one, Red."

"So what actually brings you by at the crack of dawn on a Sunday?"

He ignored my morning reference. He knew me well. One woman's crack of dawn was another man's the day's been underway for hours already.

"I wanted to see you. How are you? Sleep okay?"

I nodded and sipped soda. "What's going on with the case?"

"Parker is finishing up at the Big House. She'll be out of there shortly. The Captain wanted to make sure the scene was cleared immediately."

"I appreciate that. And you? What are you doing with the case?"

"Not a lot to be done today. Paperwork mostly."

I stared at him. He stared at me.

Seconds ticked by, then a full minute.

"Son of a b," I said. "You arrested Chef Carmichael."

He didn't respond.

"Officially arrested him? With handcuffs and fingerprints and a mugshot and he's now locked in a cell?"

"Until arraignment."

"You actually got a judge to give you an arrest warrant? On a Sunday?"

"Late last night. So on a Saturday."

"Nick Ransom, what the hell?" I thrust my drink at him, holding it out stiff-armed as if it was poisoned. "You thought a Pepsi would smooth over the fact that you're moving on Chef Carmichael way too soon? It's barely been twelve hours. There's been no investigation. Nothing. How can you do this? Just jump to conclusions? Jump the gun? Jump on the bandwagon?"

"The bandwagon?"

"Yes, the I-saw-a-man-near-the-body-so-obviously-he-killed-her-no-need-to-spend-two-hours-investigating-let's-arrest-him-case-closed bandwagon."

Ransom sipped his coffee. "He confessed."

"He what?"

"He confessed."

"To what? He did not admit to killing Lola Carmichael because he did not kill Lola Carmichael."

"He did. He confessed—"

"Stop saying confessed," I said.

"He said he killed her. Last night. Afternoon actually, before we even got to the station."

I lowered my outstretched paper cup. "He couldn't have."

"He did," Ransom repeated. "And then he professed his guilt again during questioning. I told him to get an attorney, and we processed him."

"But he didn't do it. He couldn't have," I repeated.

"People don't confess to crimes they didn't commit. Not in a death penalty state." Ransom stepped closer and kissed my forehead. "I'm sorry, Red."

I took another long gulp of my sugary beverage as Ransom walked to his silver racer, a McLaren Roadster, parked in the driveway next door. He was also my neighbor. Which often hampered the discreet part of my discreet inquiries. Most folks wanted their indiscretions kept out of the papers. I also tried to keep them out of Ransom's case files.

He fired up the engine and drove up the lane toward the guarded gate.

"Well, crap," I said to myself. "I did not see that coming."

Back in the Mini, I drove as slowly as I could, even slower than the posted fifteen MPH sign, trying to drag out the two-mile drive from my cottage to the Big House. Both of which were nestled inside Oyster Cove Plantation. Sea Pine Island called its ritzier housing communities "plantations" and each usually contained golf courses, tennis courts, and retired law enforcement folks in security uniforms who kindly raised the entry gate if you offered the proper credentials.

A smattering of cars peppered the Big House parking lot. I didn't see Jane's convertible, which brought a slight relief. I did not want to tell her about Chef's arrest after the fit she pitched yesterday. I didn't want to be there at all. But I had to oversee cleanup until the last bit of crime scene tape was removed. Vivi and Edward would be mortified. Thank the tiny baby Jesus for small favors. The garish yellow murder tape was in the back, out of sight.

The foyer was quiet as I walked to my office. It used to be the music room when the entire Big House was the Ballantyne residence. With over twenty thousand square feet in the Big House, the Ballantynes opted to convert the first floor to the Foundation's offices. A decision I appreciated every day. My floor-to-ceiling windows were dressed in white plantation shutters and fresh flowers from the garden graced my desk.

The Sunday issue of the *Islander Post* sat center next to a vase of pale pink peonies. The headline verbatim to the one Tate mumbled whilst dialing 911: *The Luck of the Ballantyne: It's All Bad Luck.*

I tossed it straight into the trash basket without another glance just as my phone rang. The desk one. On a Sunday. I clutched the receiver with one hand, held my knotted stomach with the other, and answered.

"Elliott! My dear! Can you hear me?" Edward Ballantyne bellowed into the phone as if we were using 1940s walkie-talkies from across town.

"I'm here, sir," I bellowed back, even though the line was as clear as spring water.

"What an awful set of circumstances," he said. "That poor sweet Lola Carmichael. Vivi is heartbroken."

I couldn't bring myself to say I was the one who insisted Lola come to the party on Vivi's behalf. "I know, sir. It's been awful. I feel awful." My knotted stomach gave another twist. "I can't believe she's gone."

"We're coming home early," Mr. Ballantyne said. "Vivi is too distraught to attend the rest of the summit. She feels helpless, dear Elliott, and she needs to do something for the family."

"She's looked forward to this for so long, sir. And the children will be so disappointed. Let me take care of this." Vivi had worked three solid months preparing for the Sea Life Summit in Greenland. She was hosting a children's outing to raise awareness for displaced marine animals on the final day of the conference. Still four days away. Pile that on top of the fact I told Lola to come to the party, it was too much. "Lola's only family was her daughter, Lucy. We were close. I can take care of her. I'll do whatever I can to help, I promise. Please, sir. I can do this."

"Well, let me talk to Vivi. Hold a moment, dear." His voice sounded muffled, his hand likely over most of the receiver.

I scrolled through my rolodex while I waited, flipping through paper cards until I got to Lucy Carmichael. She shared a card with Lola. The same phone number. I knew Lucy before teenagers carried their own cell phones, before Lucy ever left home. And I'd never updated it.

Carla tiptoed into my office with a vintage Crock-Pot and a stack of dollar store paper bowls. She set them on the edge of the sideboard next to my office door. "The last one. No one claimed it, I'm thinking maybe it was Chef's? I don't want that bad juju in my kitchen."

"Elliott! Are you there?"

"Yes, sir, I'm here," I said as Carla snuck out.

"It's splendid of you to help Lucy, we both think so. Vivi reminded me you two were inseparable as kids. No better offer of comfort than for you to spend time with her. Vivi says as long as you can stand in her place there, we'll stay here. We'll fly home directly after the children's outing."

"Absolutely. I'm honored. Please tell her I will take care of this and send her my love."

"Very good, then. Now what's this I hear about Chef Carmichael's arrest?"

Mr. Ballantyne might be three thousand miles away, but he knew the island's happenings practically as they happened. "Chef confessed, sir. I'm still processing. Both Lola's passing and Chef's confession."

"I can't believe Chef would harm anyone. It doesn't sound right to me. How about you, my dear?"

"Not to me either." I grabbed a notebook from my bottom drawer. "I'm already working on it, assuming there's much more to this tragedy."

"Agreed. Please give our regards to his family as well. We'll leave this in your hands." He lowered his voice. "Thank you, my dear Elliott. Vivi needs to keep busy. She's not as strong as she used to be. Knowing you're there brings us both solace. Take care of yourself. We'll see you Friday morning."

"Yes, sir, looking forward to it," I said, but he was already gone. I missed them terribly, and the reminder that Vivi wasn't as strong as she used to be scared me. The seventy-two-year-old dynamo devoted her life to helping those in need, but with each passing year, she aged faster, walked slower, and tired much too quickly.

I plucked the Lola/Lucy card from its spot in the spindle. I actually didn't know if Lucy was Lola's only family. I knew the trailer park was her family, but that's not saying much. I paged through the cards again, finding one marked Fisher's Landing. It, too, listed Lola Carmichael, and nothing else. I arranged both cards in the center of my desk. Two cards I'd barely even glanced at in the last fifteen years.

Voices from the hall pulled me from my reverie. Ballantyne staff and board members. Snippets of muffled conversations echoed in my office. "I still can't believe it." "Did you know her?" "In the Zen garden of all places." "Won't be meditating there anytime soon."

With a slow step, I left my office and walked through the back patio doors. I couldn't go farther than the front edge of the pool. Gardeners with spray hoses washed the grass while landscapers with whirring machines trimmed the edges. The smells of tangy cut grass and blooming lilacs colored the air and I wanted no part of its fresh heralding of spring. I ignored the people near the Zen garden and went back to my office.

Carla slipped in behind me, Tod on her heels. They came bearing breakfast croissants and fresh pressed mango lemonade. "Here, sweetie," Carla said. "Don't forget to eat."

Words that have never once been uttered to me before. But she was right. It was already eleven, and other than several long swigs of Pepsi, I'd yet to nibble, bite, or nip at a speck of food.

They plopped into the chairs facing my desk whilst I picked at the flaky croissant.

"Deidre mentioned that Lieutenant Handsome arrested Chef Carmichael," Tod said. His appearance back to its normal sheveled from yesterday's disheveled. "Dare I ask why?"

"It was the knife in his hand," Carla said.

"Obvs," Tod said with a mild eye roll. "I meant why he killed her."

They looked to me. A board full of the island's most assorted characters generated a nearly constant state of rumor grinding, something I learned in my earliest days. I'd become quite adept at tempering the chinwagging of the nosiest of parkers. Half of my job was keeping the rumor mill shut down. However, the murder of a local on the Big House grounds rendered the rumor mill unshutdownable.

"Ransom didn't say why Chef killed her," I said. "Just that he confessed. Case closed."

"Shut. Up." Tod leaned forward. "He flat out confessed?"

"What else could he do? His goose was cooked. Something even a half-baked chef like Carmichael could recognize." Carla looked at me as I stopped eating my croissant mid-chew. "Sorry, chicken. But maybe 'case closed' is a good thing."

I dry swallowed with a gulp. "None of this is a good thing."

"Bright side," Tod added. "Everyone from the board decided to pitch in. Arrived before the sun rose this morning." He crossed his legs and sat back. "First time that's happened since we offered free champagne at the sunrise egg roll seven Easters ago."

"Even Jane?" I asked. "I didn't see her car out front."

"Fine. Not everyone from the board," Tod said. "Close enough."

"I haven't heard from her since yesterday when she and Zibby went on the hunt for the Winnebago. Maybe she had an auction this morning?" Jane Walcott Hatting spent more than half her time in Savannah, a leisurely thirty-minute drive off the island. Jane served as president of their historical association and of her own high-end antiques auction house.

"Nope, the next auction is scheduled in two weeks," Tod said. "Didn't you get the invitation?"

Before I could answer, Corporal Parker knocked on the doorframe. "You got a minute, Elliott?"

Carla scooped up my plate of crumbs and she and Tod skedaddled out of my office. Making a show of it. I'd guess they were likely within earshot on the other side.

"I have a short list of people I still need to interview," Parker said, opening her notebook. "It's imperative we get these on the books. Two members of the board I didn't see here this morning, I'm concerned—"

I interrupted her with a small lie before she got any further. "Jane had an auction this morning. She's quite sorry she couldn't be here and sends her apologies. I'll make arrangements for her to run by the station tomorrow first thing."

"She's not on my list. She already gave a statement early this morning."

"Jane went to the police station?"

"Yep."

"Huh."

Parker rattled off two names and I directed her to the kitchen. It was nearly time for lunch and Carla would be making a daily spread. Nothing pleased board members (or any person near the Big House) more than the daily spread. It involved homemade cooking, from dressings to desserts.

"The scene is clear and everything accounted for," Parker said. "We removed the tape. I didn't like seeing it here anymore than you did. I'm really sorry about this one."

Not everything was accounted for. After she left, I walked over to the sideboard where Carla had left the old slow cooker. It was a vintage model, at least from the seventies, the faded words "Crock-Pot" still visible on the side.

"That was Lola's."

I turned to see a young woman, early thirties, in blue jeans and dusty boots, leaning against the doorframe, holding a pair of long cord leashes. Colonel Mustard and Mrs. White danced around her feet.

"Lucy!" I ran over and hugged her, a tight embrace of love and loss and sadness and joy for my old friend.

Her arms half-wrapped around me and there was no squeeze. More of a mild pat lasting a mere two seconds. "My mom bought that at a yard sale in Summerton," Lucy said, gesturing at the Crock-Pot. "I was maybe seven years old. She made nearly every meal in that thing. The special ones, anyway. She taught me to make corned beef and cabbage for St. Pat's Day. Her favorite holiday."

"Come in, come in." I half pulled her to the sofa and patted the seat as if talking to a small child. The pugs saw it as encouragement and did their darnedest to jump up to the cushions. Like cats, they tried to scale the sofa wall.

"I'm so sorry, Lucy. I wanted to call you personally, to tell you, but I don't have your number anymore."

"Harry called me. I drove straight through from Dallas last night."

"You know Dr. Fleet?"

"Sure. He taught a seminar at the college when I was in training. He keeps in touch."

A small pang hit my heart. Grumpy old Harry Fleet, crankier than Delroy Lindo in *Get Shorty*, kept in touch with Lucy, and I didn't even know she lived in Dallas. Or when she moved there. Or what she was training for.

Lucy reached down and scratched at the baby ears of Mrs. White, the tiny tags on her white collar rattling with each rub. "I met with the attorney this morning. The pugs are for Vivi."

"Oh Lucy, we can't take your pugs. They were your mother's. She loved them. You have to keep them."

"It's in the will. She wanted Vivi to care for them."

"Vivi is traveling," I said, bargaining for her to keep these creatures her mother so clearly adored.

"Then they are for you." She handed me the leashes. They weren't the simple put-your-hand-through-the-loop kind. These were fancy plastic contraptions with a click button and release switch to lengthen and shorten the leash at will.

Lucy's detached tone softened as she added, "My mom wanted Vivi to have them. I can respect her wishes and so can you."

"Of course," I said. "I'll care for them until Vivi returns. It'll be an honor."

Lucy straightened up, leaning back against a cushion. "Lola added Colonel Mustard and Mrs. White to her will when she visited her attorney on Saturday."

I noted Lucy's choice of name for her mother. Sometimes Lola, sometimes mom. To create distance? Or perhaps that was their bond. More guilt crowded in at this stranger of a girl I once knew who now looked so tough and sad, exhausted and shocked.

"Your mom changed her will on Saturday? Was that coincidental or did she worry about something? Or someone, like Chef Carmichael?"

"Nothing nefarious, Jupiter Jones. Lola was worried about having to file a bankruptcy on the Fisher's Landing. Things were getting wonky around there."

"I knew about the almost bankruptcy, but I assumed she skipped the visit to her attorney's office. She was at the party." I blanched when I mention Lola and the party. "I'm sorry, Lucy. About your mom and the party and Chef—"

"No way my uncle killed my mother. They got along really well. No beef."

"But she said she had a falling out with the Carmichael Clan."

"My dad and my grandmother," Lucy said. "Virginia. The matriarch of the Carmichaels. She's a tough nut."

"Could Chef have paid off the trailer park for Lola? Maybe it created tension between them. Perhaps this was a money dispute that heated up?"

"I don't think so," Lucy said. "My uncle liked my mom, but not three hundred and eighty-seven thousand dollars liked her, you know? Even with all his success, I don't think he has an extra four hundred k he won't miss."

"But you don't know for sure?"

"Not technically," she answered with a shrug.

We fell into an odd but comfortable space. Talking as if it were a typical investigative case rather than Lucy coping with the murder of her mother at the hands of her uncle.

Mrs. White had nearly made it to the top cushion of the sofa. I gave her a lift and she promptly barked at Colonel Mustard. I didn't speak puppy, but it sounded suspiciously like "I win."

"Someone paid off the mortgage," I said. "Coincidence? Lola's killed shortly thereafter?" At Lucy's silence, I added, "Maybe family is clouding your judgment?"

"Why isn't it clouding yours?"

"Chef isn't family," I said.

"Close enough. He's been dating Jane for years. She's the

chair of your board. That's like family."

"What?" I sat up straight and rattled the clunky yellow and white leash boxes.

"Besides, my uncle didn't kill my mother. My dad did and I'm sticking around to prove it."

"Let the professionals take care of this, Lucy."

"I am. I've had my PI license for nine years."

"You're a private investigator?"

"Yes, ma'am. In Dallas, Texas," she said with an exaggerated drawl and a tip of an imaginary cowboy hat. "Remember our first case? Been the only thing I've ever wanted to do. I tried college, took some classes, then started an internship with a small investigative firm. As in one guy working out of an office above a psychic's office. We're actually still there."

"That's amazing, Lucy. Congratulations." Not sure why I said that, since it wasn't as if she'd just graduated and she'd been at it almost a decade. I cleared my throat and leaned in. "Let me help."

"No offense, but this isn't the case of the chipped coffee mug. I've been at this longer, and I surpassed your abilities before my twenty-fifth birthday. I've got this."

"You're not licensed to practice in South Carolina."

"Neither are you."

I felt affronted she knew of my current PI status and still doubted my ability. I shifted on the sofa cushion and changed my tone. "Why would your dad kill your mom?"

"That's what I'm going to figure out."

"Why do you think he did it?"

She shrugged. "I don't know. Other than he's the only person my uncle would lie to protect."

"That's a pretty big lie. You do remember we're a death penalty state?"

She bent down to scratch Colonel Mustard's back.

"So you're going to prove your father killed your mother to save your uncle?"

"Family, right?" Lucy sighed. "Look, Lola owned Fisher's Landing until her death when it would then revert to my dad. My guess? He needed the money. He'll sell the park, pocket the cash, and drive off into the sunset."

"I don't mean to sound accusatory, but how did Lola get so far behind in payments?"

"Nothing to accuse. Rentals aren't what they used to be. Mom was a softie. She always let people slide on payments. Not everyone there could afford it."

That's saying something when a person couldn't afford the rent at a trailer park. The two sides of life on Sea Pine Island. Those barely scratching out a living at a trailer park and those barely carving out time to visit their twenty-million-dollar waterfront third home.

"Your dad needed money? Do you know what for?"

"He always needed money."

"And he's violent?"

Lucy half-laughed and stood, setting Mrs. White on the hardwood floor next to Colonel Mustard. "Nope. He could sweet talk a dog out of a pork chop." She dug into her pocket and pulled out a wrinkled business card, then walked to my desk to grab a pen. "Here's my cell. I'm staying at the park in the rental next door to mom's." She faced me. "I can't go in Lola's trailer."

"So you do want my help?"

"No offense, but you'll only get in my way. But you could come to the wake. It'll be Tuesday at Tug's."

"Already? Are you pushing yourself too soon?"

"It's St. Patrick's Day. What better day to celebrate my mom?" Lucy walked back to the pugs, rubbed their backsides while they chewed their beef sticks. "Come to Tug's. Lola really liked you and the Ballantynes. She'd want you there."

I felt sick. That's almost exactly what I said to Lola. *Vivi would want you there.* And it got her killed.

Lucy said goodbye to Colonel Mustard and Mrs. White, then picked up the Crock-Pot, tucking the dollar store paper bowls inside.

"Lucy, I'm so sorry," I said softly.

Lucy didn't slow her pace. She quietly left my office without a glance back.

FIVE

(Day #2: Sunday Afternoon)

I hooked the leash containers beneath the leg of the side table next to the sofa and walked down to Jane's office. Once the parlor room at the front corner of the Big House, it was furnished with teak furniture and lovely silk wallpapers and overlooked the English rose garden that ran along the side of the house.

My intention was to leave Jane a note, but I encountered the woman herself.

"Jane, you're here."

"I'm aware of that, Elliott." Her straight bob fell into place with each snap of her sarcastic head. "But more importantly, I need to talk to you."

"And I need to ask about you and Chef Carmichael."

"He didn't do it. He could not, and would not, have done this horrible thing. I have no idea why they arrested him."

"Because Chef confessed."

"What does that have to do with anything? Obviously he's lying."

"You're hardly an impartial character witness," I said. "You and Chef have been dating for years?"

"My private life is private. Hence the word private. Shall we delve into your private life?"

"It's not relevant."

"Really? Because your private life just arrested my private life." Jane grabbed a silver Tiffany pen and began tapping it. Sharp, rhythmic taps. I stared down at her, she tapped and stared back at me. "Shall we continue?"

"I'm here to help, Jane. We're going to have to work together." I sat in one of the high back chairs facing her desk. "Why would Chef confess? Could he be protecting his brother? Do you know why would he do that?"

"Family, of course."

"Not *of course*, Jane. I wasn't all that close to my family, but how close do you need to be to volunteer for the death penalty? It has to be more than just 'he's family.' It must be some kind of debt he's owed."

"Not necessarily. It can be family. If it was Edward? Or Vivi? Would you volunteer then?"

"In a blink." I'd do anything for the Ballantynes. I owed them so much, but none of that mattered. Confessing to protect them would not be so I could repay a debt. I simply couldn't live if either were locked up. Or worse. On death row.

"You have to help him," Jane said.

"It's tricky. This is not a simple decision."

"Yes, it is. He's innocent. Decision made."

"Let's say I prove him innocent. That means the man he's trying to sacrifice his life for, his brother, is now on trial, with the possibility of the death penalty. Chef Carmichael would never forgive me. And by me, I mean you."

"I can't let him do this," Jane said. Her matter-of-fact demeanor cracked ever so slightly. "And I can't stop him."

"Probably no chance he'll talk to me? Help me prove he didn't do it?"

"None. That's why he confessed. He does not want an investigation by anyone."

"Why does Chef think his brother killed Lola? Is there any motive? A reason his brother would Winnebago his way into to town and stab his ex-wife in the middle of a huge event? Anything he told you or you overheard or you can think up?"

"No. Nothing. Tom doesn't share his intimate life details with the whole island. He rarely talks about his family, which by extension includes Lola." She tapped her pen against the soft blotter cover on her desk. "Now you can't just sit around my office philosophizing. He's rushing through the process to get a hearing."

"Arraignments usually move quickly anyway. It'll probably be tomorrow, Tuesday at the latest."

"Not arraignment, Elliott. Sentencing. He's pleading guilty, waiving trial and jury. Gregory Mead is his attorney. He's trying to slow Tom down, get him some kind of a deal, but Tom is trying to speed it up. Gregory says it'll be next Monday, one week from tomorrow. If not sooner."

"Tell Chef it looks suspicious that he's rushing. It'll trigger the investigation he's trying to prevent. Better yet, I'll tell him. Set it up with his attorney and I'll be there."

"Is that true?" Jane asked, almost hopeful. "His haste will help him? Lieutenant Obvious might actually try to find the real person who did this?"

"Obvious is the key. Ransom has the confession of the man holding the murder weapon over the dead body. It's open and shut."

"Chef will never meet with you. He wants it this way." Jane's face turned sour, almost scared. "It's over for him. His career, his restaurant. His life."

I didn't fully understand why Chef Carmichael was moving so quickly and a shortened timeline ran against me. I'd worked some ugly cases in my career as PI-in-training slash charity director, but this case didn't have a lot of dark corners for me to explore. Like she said, open and shut. "In a week?"

"I told you. Stop philosophizing. Start solving."

Jane returned to her notes and I walked toward the door.

"Thank you," Jane said quietly.

I turned back to say you're welcome, but before I could form the first syllable, Jane glared at me. "Now, Elliott. I meant now."

While I was gone, the puppy fairy had popped by my office. Next to Colonel Mustard and Mrs. White sat a crate, a pet carrier, bags of toys, food, dishes and poop bags, and a note written in a chunky scrawl: *They're potty-trained, but will chew anything.*

I immediately called Sid. "You ever own a pair of pugs?"

"I've never owned a pair of anything living," Sid said. "You just curious?"

"I inherited Lola's pugs. Temporarily, anyway. Until Vivi returns on Friday."

"That's only five days. You'll be fine."

"Sure, sure." I thought about the busy week ahead of me. What did I do with pugs? "Do I need a sitter or a nanny or something?"

Sid laughed.

"Can I leave them at my house?"

"Probably."

"Can I leave them at your house?"

"Definitely not."

Sid offered no advice at all. She lived her life free of children and pets, too, and apparently I was going to need to figure this out on my own. Me and my friend Google.

They played in my office (only chewing part of the sofa leg) while I finished my work at the Big House. When the day turned quiet, I gathered up their goodies, making three trips to the Mini to get it all in. With a single scoop, I carried them to the car and drove the whole carload to my cottage. After an hour of unloading, setting up, and searching all of the internet to figure out how much to feed and water them, we all settled into an early dinner. I calmly ate a bowl of cereal over the sink whilst they snarfled up two separate but equal bowls of crunchies. It sounded like a pig farm at feeding time, but two happier pugs in shin-deep food could not be found. Food splatters dotted the floor, wall, cabinets, their faces, and color-coordinated collars.

They barked and nipped, taking turns jumping and biting at the hem of my shorty pants until I grabbed their leashes. We walked on the beach. I discovered how handy those little poop bags could really be when they each made two deposits on the sand. Forty-five minutes later when we were all sufficiently tired, we tucked in for the night. I set the crate up in the corner of my room, but placed the puppies on the bed with me. I pulled out my notebook and they cuddled together on my pillow.

I wrote two names at the top of a clean page: Lola Carmichael and Chef Carmichael.

Do I help or do I not help?

Pro: Lucy needs my help, even though she didn't ask.

Con: Ransom will have a shit fit.

Pro: Jane asked for my help, even though she rarely has faith in me.

Con: Ransom will have a shit fit.

Pro: Vivi asked me to help and I'll do anything for her.

Con: Ransom will just have to deal with it.

I outlined a list of questions of the standard investigative variety, almost like a form. I made a mental note: I needed to create investigative forms. Start a system, keep myself organized. Until then, I used a pad of paper.

Who killed Lola? Why kill Lola? Why kill her at the Ballantyne's party? Circumstance or convenience?

Where to start? That was the easiest. Right where Lola wanted me to start: Who paid off her mortgage?

I scrambled downstairs for the packet Lola had given me at her trailer. It felt as if weeks had gone by rather than a single day. Back in bed with the snoring pugs, I spread the papers on the bed. The original mortgage was written through Charter Bank. It was all in order with a payment schedule and proper signatures. But the folder also held several late notices. Half threatening, half not. Corporate severity mixed with Southern flexibility. Bring current or foreclosure proceedings will ensue, kindly call to make arrangements. Not from a bureaucratic no-name call center, but someone local and personal: Chas Obermeyer as signatory on behalf of the bank. The Vice President of Charter Bank was Lola's banker?

A stroke of luck for me and my investigation. Chas was on the Ballantyne board. Not one of my most ardent supporters or most cooperative members, but I was pretty confident he wouldn't slam the door in my face.

I jotted down another interesting detail. Chas's wife's pink car was at Tug's yesterday, parked in the empty lot when I left with the marlin. Then I wondered if it was actually an interesting detail or perhaps a normal detail on an island where you see someone you know every time you don your flip flops.

A note on a ripped piece of paper was paperclipped to one of the delinquent notices. Handwritten in loopy scrawl, Lola Carmichael gave me, Elliott Lisbon, permission to look at her banking information.

She had wanted me to do this on Monday, and now I needed to do that and so much more. I traced her signature with my finger and vowed to see this through. Lola probably had ten dozen things she wanted accomplished before she died, but I only knew this one. It may not have been her actual dying wish, but to me it was.

I turned the page of my notebook and created a timeline. Chef Carmichael's sentencing was in eight days, one week from tomorrow. The Suffrage Society's Woman of the Year Seaside Brunch was in five days. My closest friend, Sid Bassi, top realtor and leading hospice volunteer, was their president, and my board chair, Jane Walcott Hatting, all-round head of everything, was their honoree. And my surrogate mother, Vivi Ballantyne, kindest woman ever to grace the state of South Carolina, was flying home that morning.

Meaning my timeline just shrunk from eight days to five. No way could I let Vivi arrive in the middle of the melee. This needed to be wrapped up. For her and for Lola.

I gathered up the mortgage papers and stuffed them back into the packet envelope, set it on the nightstand with my notebook on top, and clicked off the light, leaving the two puppies to not-so-softly snore next to me.

"What's five days?" I whispered to my new roommates. I'd never had a bigger problem or a shorter deadline, but I was up for the challenge. Because Miss Carmichael hadn't been killed in the conservatory with a candlestick. She'd been stabbed to death in my own backyard.

SIX

(Day #3: Monday Morning)

My normal morning routine was now expanded by approximately thirty-seven minutes. The time it took to feed, water, clean up the feed and water, then walk Colonel Mustard and Mrs. White. I tacked on another ten minutes to toss, pull, and squeak toys with them. I didn't know standard playing times for pugs. Or a set of puppies. Internet articles ranged, but most said an hour. Who had that kind of time? Probably those who didn't run charities while solving crimes. I played with them not nearly long enough, and they barked at me to let me know, but I did need to leave the house. I had a committee meeting at the Big House after lunch, but my morning was free. Free to start figuring things out.

Sea Pine Island was shaped like a short boot. Harborside Plantation was located at the southern tip of its boot toe, and the bridge to mainland South Carolina was located at the top of its out-of-date ankle laces. Cabana Boulevard, the main road, started down in Harborside and wound its way up through palm trees, crape myrtles, and traffic lights across the island and over the Palmetto Bridge into Summerton, South Carolina. Oyster Cove Plantation, gated homestead to my cottage and the Big House, was close to the ankle laces.

I drove south on Cabana to about mid-island, then turned into the drive of a squat building with palms, both planted and potted, decorating the lot. The words "Charter Bank" were decaled on the glass in gold letters. I didn't have an appointment, but was hoping I didn't need one. The doors had barely been open five minutes and I was the only one to enter.

I smoothed my breezy linen tunic, slightly wrinkled from the drive, but still looking snazzy enough to wear to a bank since I paired it with Vans instead of flip flops. Chas Obermeyer's assistant, Ann, sat at her desk on the far side of the open room. I said good morning and asked if Chas was available.

She perkily told me Chas was booked all morning.

I sat in the padded chair next to her desk and leaned in as if I was about to divulge nuclear key codes.

"Ann, we've had a tragedy at the Ballantyne over the weekend," I said in a low tone.

"I heard," she said. "It's simply awful. Lola was one of my favorite customers. She brought me ambrosia salad on my birthday last month."

"Lola was kind and thoughtful and I'm here to talk to Chas about her. Certainly you can sneak me five minutes this morning."

She peeked over her shoulder at his closed door. "He absolutely hates going off-schedule."

"This is a special circumstance. Even Chas would agree," I said. "And his first appointment can't be here, I'm the only car in the front lot."

"True..." She glanced toward the glass doors. "Mrs. Quattlebaum hasn't arrived..."

"I promise I won't be but five minutes. Ten tops."

She looked from the closed office to the entrance doors, then made a quick note on the pad in front of her and stood. "For Lola."

She knocked once on Chas's door, then opened it for me to enter. I thanked her and she shut it behind me.

"Elliott?" Chas said. "Are you on my calendar this morning? I think I would've known that."

"Not exactly. I'm here about Lola Carmichael. I have a couple questions and then I'll be on my way."

His phone beeped and he flipped it over in his hand, thumb-tapping faster than a grade-schooler. Chas Obermeyer looked as if he was once athletic, perhaps the high school cornerback, maybe even college second-string. Now slightly soft, slightly balding, slightly overfilling the snug suit he wore. His office was decorated in community award plaques and pictures with officials. A foam-core architectural drawing in one corner, the requisite island painting on an easel in the other.

"What do you need, Elliott?" Chas looked up from his phone. "I'm booked all day."

"It's Lola's mortgage on Fisher's Landing." I handed him the packet of papers. "Lola said she was behind on payments until a surprise benefactor paid her mortgage in full."

"And?"

"And she wanted to know who the benefactor was. She asked me to help find out."

Chas stood with the packet unopened in his hands. "I can't help you. There are privacy laws. Our Ballantyne connection does not supersede them, if that's what you're thinking."

"Not at all what I was thinking. I have Lola's permission. There's a formal letter inside that envelope."

He cracked open the flap and pulled out the scratch paper. "It's dated Saturday. This past Saturday. The day she died. Interesting timing."

"We spoke that morning. Before she…before she came to the Big House. She had serious concerns about her mortgage."

"You think this is why she was killed? Carmichael killed her over her mortgage? You really need to more careful about who you let associate with the Ballantyne."

"We don't know why anyone killed her." I put up my hand before he could argue an argument I wanted no part of. It was too soon to talk about Lola in such a cold way. "Let's keep it simple. She wanted to know who paid off her mortgage. You can certainly tell me that. I have permission."

"This is hardly legal," he said, slipping the note back into the packet.

"Hardly legal doesn't mean not legal."

He stared at me a beat, then sat and started tapping on his keyboard. "You owe me for this. Something big. A serious favor." He tapped and waited, tapped and waited. He finally hit two keys with flourish. "Ah, right. I'll tell you what I told her. I can't identify who deposited the money for the payoff. It was paid with a cashier's check. The person provided no identification. The balance paid in full."

"I practically knew all that already. That's what she told me. Some unknown person paid it off."

"That's what happened."

"Then why do I owe you anything for that non-information?"

"I do my job, you do yours." He handed me back the envelope. "I'm sorry she's gone. Really. I always liked her."

He sounded mostly sincere, but the Obermeyers traveled in the golf club and ladies lunch crowd, not the trailer park and bingo parlor crowd. Which made Bitsy's car at Tug Boat Slim's Saturday morning even stranger.

"There's nothing else you can divulge? You must know of an odd detail or a random statistic?"

"One minor thing. Either she was mistaken or you were, but the entire mortgage wasn't paid off. Only the outstanding balance. She still has seven years left on the mortgage. Or did.

Well, someone does. Guess it's up to probate now."

"That's not much, but I'll take it."

He tapped two more keys and placed his folded hands square on the desk.

"You must have been close to be her personal banker," I said.

"Not close, but I do try to get to know all of our long-term clients."

"And Bitsy? Was she close to Lola?"

"Bitsy?" He asked with two raised brows. "I doubt she even knew her."

I tucked the packet into my bag and thought maybe Bitsy really was at Tug's for the crab bisque.

Except they were closed on Saturday morning to compete at the Irish Spring.

That thought kept me preoccupied on the short drive up Cabana and then down Washburn Lane toward the Intracoastal Waterway and Fisher's Landing. The dead end street was abuzz with activity. Boats and banners and colorful flags flapping in the wind. The lot at Tug Boat Slim's was starting to fill up, but for once I skipped that tiny area and parked on the dirt path in front of Lola's.

Her trailer was the third from the entrance, with the first two seemingly in a battle for most manmade lawn ornaments gathered in one place. One single wide was faded turquoise, the other faded Pepto pink. Both had enough plastic flamingos, mirror balls, spinning daisies, gnomes, flags, and wire chickens to be seen from space.

Clearly neither was the rental Lucy was staying in. More likely she was in the old yellow one with the white stripe in spot four. There wasn't a car out front. I didn't even know what Lucy drove, but I assumed it had Texas plates. I could better help if I knew what it was. And then could steer clear whenever I saw it.

I stood in front of Lola's house, her plastic grassy meadow the same as it was two days earlier. Just two days and everything was now wrong.

In contrast to her collectible-crazed neighbors, Lola didn't have much décor out front. Giving me very few places to look for a hide-a-key. Nothing taped to the sling slats on the aluminum beach chairs, and neither terra cotta potted geranium yielded entry. I tried the trailer's rounded front door on the off-chance it might be unlocked. Island living meant unlocked doors and open windows. It was a quiet life. However, trailer park living also meant temporary hook-ups with pay-by-the-night sewer access and no ID required.

Lola was no fool and her door was locked.

Her silver Airstream was on wheels, though I doubt that sucker had moved since it was rolled into place when President Eisenhower was still in office. It had slatted windows on both sides and a large picture window on each end. The front window oversaw large propane-like tanks secured to a hitch for all the world to see. But the back window was tucked into a copse of crape myrtles and sticker bushes where no one could see.

With a casual look over my shoulder, I crept into the thick forest. I placed one foot on the rickety rear bumper of the trailer, then tested it with part of my weight. Seemed stable enough. I climbed aboard and side-stepped my way to the center. Branches whipped my face, arms, and bare ankles. Note to self: next time I go scrambling through the woodsy areas, don full-length heavy jeans, not lightweight linen shorty pants.

I patted the rusty rivets outlining the rear window, which sat flush against the frame. Not a slider to pull or a gap to pry it from its position. It must open from the inside like with a big push or crank. I cupped my hands and squinted my eyes and tried to peek through the glass, keeping my face at least an inch away from the grimy, gross, disgustingly never-washed surface.

But between the dirt-coated glass outside and some kind of window covering inside, I couldn't see a thing.

Teetering off the bumper, nearly losing my balance, I realized I was standing on the perfect hiding spot for a key. The rickety bumper covered in bramble. I gingerly inspected the space beneath the metal bumper, careful not to slice my hand open. Visions of monster tetanus shots and flesh-eating bacteria danced like black spots as I patted my way up one side and down the other. Jackpot. A slim key fell into my hand.

Using half a bottle of hand-sani (I would've used more if I had it), I cleaned up to my elbows along with the entire key, then calmly walked right up to the front/side/only door and let myself in.

The interior was surprisingly bright. Sheers covered the sunny windows. The roller shades were still rolled up at the tops, not pulled down for the night. As if Lola would return any minute.

Based on the amount of wood paneling covering all main surfaces, her trailer might have been more late sixties than fifties, but the kitsch was all mid-century, and it was everywhere.

I started in the rear. The whole trailer house was probably no longer than twenty-five feet. The rounded rear end held the bathroom, with the roller shade pulled firmly down for privacy. Lola's palettes of shadows, blushers, and lipsticks covered the narrow sink shelf while jars of cold creams, body lotions, and perfume bottles sat on a standing tv dinner tray.

Back in the kitchen/living area, I checked the overhead cabinets. The doors slid open to reveal their treasures. Board games and books. A random selection of Alfred Hitchcock and Three Investigators mysteries. Likely the ones I'd shared with Lucy so many years earlier. I didn't know if I was happy she kept them or disappointed she didn't take them with her when she left home. I took down a tattered box of *Clue* and a vintage Mahjong set, the tiles chipped and faded, but carefully placed in rows inside.

The two-burner white enamel stove still held a large pot, clean, with two wooden spoons resting inside. Packages of dry mustard, parsley, and thyme were next to a chef's knife. I checked the trash. A fresh wrapper for beef brisket, plus carrot and onion stubs. All the fixings one would need to make a pot of corned beef and cabbage.

The fridge was no larger than something you'd haul to a tailgate and was filled with homemade everything, including leftover green pretzel salad in a clear CorningWare dish. All created in a kitchen no bigger than the trailer's bathroom. And let me tell you, I'd peeked into the water closet in the back and it was no larger than a linen closet in a 1970s single wide. Apparently my every small space metaphor involved mobile homes. I couldn't imagine anything tinier. Perhaps half a loft in SoHo? Some kind of roadside motel room?

I sat at the dinette: a short bench with a flip-down table. The décor was fifties knickknack, but all done with care and style. Every single thing seemed to have been carefully curated, carefully placed. Instead of crammed, the compact space looked well-appointed. Lola Carmichael clearly loved her tiny house. I felt a kinship. My cottage was Goldilocks just right. I felt safe and contained and I wouldn't ever trade it.

A worn cookbook was open on the table, flipped to a recipe for corned beef and cabbage, a post-it to mark the page. Another postie tabbed to the front. I turned to it. It was the title page. I read it and nearly choked. *The Wharf's Cookery* by Chef Tom Carmichael. Signed: *For Lola, Slainte!*

The Google machine on my phone returned an answer to my query in two point seven seconds. *Slainte!* was Gaelic for "good health," an Irish toast of cheers. It sounded friendly. But that was before Lola may have used Chef's recipe at the Ballantyne's Irish Spring Pot of Gold Cook-Off. He'd won that contest nearly every year we held it. Perhaps he saw her enter the contest and lost his mind. It was paper thin as far as motives went, but people killed for less every day. Though maybe not much less than a corned beef recipe. On Saturday, we'd never reached the contest part of the party, the part where people tasted the pots of gold. Where people would notice if Chef and Lola used the same recipe. Her crock was empty and in my office when I first saw it. I made a mental note to check if Carla had tasted Lola's corned beef.

Several shiny brochures were tucked beneath the cookbook. A fancy development with boat slips, sailing club, condos, and villas. Was Lola moving? Maybe she was going to sell the park. But how do you do that with a bankruptcy over your head? A bankruptcy usually meant a fire sale, which would not net leftover cash to live in luxury. Besides, I'd always thought Lola loved this place.

I tapped the brochures on the wobbly table and stood. A picture of Lola and Lucy hung on the wall near the door. Lola's arm around Lucy, squeezing her close. Lucy caught mid-laugh. "Oh, Lola. Why would Chef Carmichael hurt you? Why would anyone?"

The door rattled as someone knocked. I jumped back, smacking my elbow on one of the tiny oven knobs. I shoved the brochures into my bag, grabbed what had to be a rubber chew toy from the counter, and calmly opened the door.

"I just needed a toy—" I stopped mid-sentence once I realized it wasn't Parker or Ransom here to arrest me for breaking and entering.

A woman in rollers stood three feet below on the astro grass. "Are you basting a turkey?" she asked.

I glanced down at the obvious squishy end to a baster and

tossed it back on the counter. I stepped down to join her.

"I'm Imogene Metwally," she said and held out her hand, the worst habit ever introduced into polite society. "Lola's best friend since the day I moved in."

I kindly shook her hand and calculated how many minutes I needed to wait before I could use hand-sani without offense. Turned out I only needed thirteen seconds and a good excuse.

I led her to the seating area on the lawn. I made a big show about the dirt on the side of the chair and commenced with a quick sani swash. "I'm Elliott Lisbon with the Ballantyne Foundation."

"Of course. I recognized you when you went inside Lola's," she said with a vague wave toward the back of the trailer park. "Well, Irene did. She called me. Probably called half the residents."

I glanced around. I bet a dozen people saw me go inside. Sets of curtains fluttered in the light breeze, trailer home to trailer home. I needed to remember that. Breaking and entering wasn't exactly covered in the PI-in-training handbook. I was writing my own.

"Lola loved your whole setup over there," Imogene said. "Talked about Mrs. Ballantyne and you and your afternoon tea socials." She sighed a sigh of the heartbroken and a set of tears ran down her face and onto her old t-shirt. "She loved your parties."

"I'm so sorry." For your loss. For hosting parties. For insisting Lola attend. For not noticing she was there until it was too late.

Imogene blew her nose into a tattered tissue. "I don't know what I'll do without her. People say that all the time, and it sounds so fake, but honestly, I've seen her nearly every day of my life. You ever have a friend like that?"

I had Sid, my closest friend. She wasn't someone I saw

every day, but I couldn't imagine my life without her.

"Lola and I used to run this island," Imogene said. "You mind if I smoke? I won't if it bugs you." She pulled a pack from the pocket of her droopy cardigan. "Those were the days."

"Please, go ahead," I said. "You must have known Jessie, then, her ex-husband?"

"Of course I know Jessie. A looker like him. He's hard to miss. Tight jeans, leather jacket, you know the type. Lola fell fast." Imogene pointed down the short street running perpendicular to Lola's lot. The tail end of an old Winnebago stuck out.

"He's here?" I said. "At Fisher's Landing?"

"You bet. Lola let him stay. He's her daughter's father. That's his usual hookup down near the end. Lola wouldn't speak to him, but he could stay."

"Lucy seems to think Jessie had something to do with Lola's death."

Imogene waved her smoking cigarette toward me. "No chance. He's a cheat, that's for dang sure, but the man could not harm a housefly. He comes in for your Irish Gold party and the Oyster Festival. Says hi to the old crowd, that kind of thing. Talks to me and my Austin."

"Is that your husband?"

"My son. A couple years younger than Lucy. Austin had the biggest crush on Lucy. Me and Lola took 'em to see the turtles hatch near every year when they were little. Boy I miss that tomgirl. Now I'll probably never see her again."

"She's in town."

"Here? Well, I guess she'd come in for the party, too. Make a family day of it. You know she called her mother twice a week? Such a good girl. But I didn't see her at the party. I wish I would've."

"She came after," I said softly.

"Oh. Right."

"You were at the party on Saturday?" I hoped I didn't sound too incredulous, but I was beginning to think I wasn't very good at my job. How did I miss so many people?

"First trip to the Big House. Helped Lola set up her station. We used the good paper cloths. Made it look real nice. I bet she would've won, too." Imogene blew her nose again. "Lola could cook circles 'round those other chefs. I would've loved to have seen their faces when she hoisted that trophy. But I couldn't stay. I had to work the lunch shift. I said goodbye to her. No, wait. I said 'see you later, hon' and left. And then she never came home."

"Hey, Ma." A kid driving a golf cart whizzed up to Lola's side lawn. "Can I take the car? I'll drop you, but we gotta go."

"Oh crap." She stomped out her cigarette and hurried to the cart, checking her rollers as if to see if her hair was dry. "Plum forgot what I was doing. Wandering around like a dotty old gal."

I joined her at the golf cart.

"This is my son, Austin," she said with obvious pride. "Honey, this is Ms. Lisbon. She runs the Ballantyne Foundation. You know, the Big House?" She nudged him. "And guess what she told me? Lucy's in town. I bet she's staying here at the park."

He looked at me for confirmation. "Really? She's here?" He touched his hair, almost subconsciously.

I think I judged too quickly when I called him a kid. Or perhaps I needed glasses. Or should actually wear the ones I already owned. Austin Metwally was late twenties, but in a beach bum kind of way. Faded tee, wrinkled cargo shorts, worn flip-flops.

"Lucy's staying at least a week," I said. "For her mother."

Austin looked at Lola's trailer. "Yeah. That can't be easy." He squeezed his mom's hand.

Silence followed. The three of us in the sun, at the edge of

Lola's plastic yard, lost in thoughts of what used to be.

Imogene took a deep breath followed by another lengthy sigh. She climbed into the golf cart, seeming much older than her years. "I got to get to work. It was really nice talking to you, Ms. Lisbon."

"Please, call me Elliott."

"Okay, then, Miss Elliott. You come by the diner sometime. Be my pleasure to have you in."

"Which diner?"

"Ida Claire. It's off Marsh Grass Road about a mile down from the Gullah Café. We got the best fried chicken and waffles in all of South Carolina."

"I'm sure—"

"Now I know your Miss Carla over at the Big House makes a fine fried chicken, but she's got nothing on Ida Claire."

With a weak wave, Austin made a zippy u-turn and drove down the narrow road toward the last row.

The park was quiet. Distant traffic and lawn mower sounds faded in and out. I crossed the road and made my way down to the old Winnebago parked three spots from the end of the short lane. A double spot. I knocked on the door, but no one answered. I walked a full circle around. The curtains were pulled closed, no chance to peek in. A tow bar stuck out prominently from the back. Perhaps he brought a car?

Two minutes later I was back inside Lola's trailer. It felt empty, not just because no one was there, but because no one would return. "I will find who did this, Lola Carmichael," I said to the lonely space, reaffirming my vow. "You wanted my help and I will not let you down."

I picked up the cookbook and locked the trailer, sliding the key into my bag. Once I tucked everything into the Mini, I snapped my belt and made my own u-turn, but toward the park's exit on Washburn Lane. I idled in the driveway. Tug's to my left, Cabana Boulevard at the end of Washburn to my right. I was debating my next destination when I noticed the hubbub across the way, barely forty feet up the road. The colorful flags and banners were there to announce the opening of the new Palmetto Bay Sailing Club. The same name from the brochures on Lola's table.

I drove over and parked near the entrance. Just as I got out, a Winnebago pulled out of Fisher's Landing. The driver glanced my way. I recognized him from the Irish Spring. At the time, I had assumed he was one of the servers. Looked like I assumed wrong. That must have been Jessie Carmichael and I never even knew it. He quickly turned away from me and steered the roaring Winnebago down the road.

At least I knew where to find him. His enormous camper chugged when it moved and the painted W was as recognizable as the Golden Arches.

It didn't occur to me until I was across the lot that he might be heading home. Wherever that might be. Could be anywhere when your house had wheels.

The Palmetto Bay sales trailer looked like a distant rich cousin to the trailer homes at Fisher's Landing. It had wood-like trim and skirting. Mock shutters bookended each window.

"Elliott Lisbon, what are you doing here?" Bitsy Obermeyer said to me.

My second surprise of the day. I was so caught up in the Winnebago, I missed the pink Mercedes parked in the lot.

"Bitsy? I didn't know you were in sales." As I said it, I noticed a large architectural drawing propped on an easel. The same one from Chas's office. "This is Chas's development?"

"Our development. Isn't it divine?" She walked over to a display box the size of a pool table. A diorama. The entire property was set out in miniature complete with sailboats and slips. "We have four condo buildings. Each home has its own personal elevator, dipping pool, and oversized lanai. Premiere Sea Pine Island living."

"I saw Chas this morning. He didn't mention this development or that it was directly across from Lola's."

"Why would he?"

"We were talking about her." Two long strides took me to the side window of the sales trailer. I stood on my tippy toes. "You can even see Lola's from here. Interesting location. A yacht club with the view of the local trailer park."

Bitsy snapped the plantation shutters closed. "Not at all. Just a view of Tug Boat's. A landmark eatery on the island. I've definitely seen Vivi Ballantyne there. If it's good enough for our local celebrity…"

"Uh-huh."

"What brings you by? Ready to trade in your tiny cottage? I'm afraid we might be out of your price range." Bitsy brightened. "Oh, but your police boyfriend is quite wealthy, right? Or the Ballantynes. Perhaps a second home? Many of our prominent island residents do that, as you well know. It's quite handy to have a condo near your house."

"I'm here because of Lola. She mentioned the Sailing Club, talked about it quite a bit. With her passing, I thought I'd check it out."

"I heard about Lola. A true tragedy." She actually tsked, but was saved from more tsking when the phone rang. "It's a sunny day at the Palmetto Bay Sailing Club, how may I help you?"

Several property renderings lined the far wall. I studied them and thought of Lola having all those brochures on her table. Was she just curious? Was she coming into money? The condo drawings had prices penciled next to them. The lowest started at half a million. How does one go from bankruptcy to luxury waterfront living? Maybe not so difficult when a stranger pays your debts. But give up Fisher's Landing? Lola was the center of that place. Like a mother in a sorority house. Maybe she'd keep both, manage it from across the street.

Bitsy cheerfully chattered about deposits and models and brunches on the deck. Nothing questionable or even curious. When she settled into her desk, phone to her ear, I threw a wave, then left the sales trailer and the Sailing Club behind me.

A two-mile drive and ten minutes later, I walked into the Big House. The foyer décor was a mishmash of St. Patrick's Day and Easter. We usually take our holidays one at a time, fully enjoying the first before embracing the second, but this year Easter fell in March which left us little time to transition. Though I doubted we would ever fully celebrate St. Patrick's Day the same again. It felt wrong to rip down the glittery green decorations now. As if we'd moved on and were trying to forget.

Lucy Carmichael stood in the foyer alone. "Hey, Lucy," I said, happy I had slid her mother's cookbook out of my bag and into my backseat before I got out of the Mini. "Nice to see you here."

She gave me a head tip as if we were surfer buds passing on the sand.

"Quick question," I said. "I didn't realize your dad stayed at Fisher's Landing while he was on the island, but I just saw him drive out. Is he leaving town?"

"Are you asking out of curiosity or as an investigator? Because if it's the latter, I already told you I don't want your help. When I do want it, I'll ask." Her hands were tucked into the back pockets of her jeans. "I'll call you. As often as you called me."

Jane clipped across the marble floor until she stood three feet from me. "What are you doing here?"

"I work here?" I said.

"This is not what you should be working on," Jane said.

"Well, she's not working on my mother's..." Lucy paused. "Case."

Jane blinked at her, then me, then back at Lucy. "We all want the same thing."

"Then we all want me to handle it," Lucy said.

I noticed Matty, Deidre Burch, and Zibby talking across the foyer next to a long table covered in decorated hats worthy of a royal wedding marching in an Easter parade at the Kentucky Derby.

"Why is everyone here for the Easter Roll meeting?" I asked. "It's not for two hours."

"It was this morning," Jane said.

"No, it's this afternoon," I said.

"I moved it," Jane said.

"You moved it?" I asked.

"Matty had an interview with a new professor at Sea Pine Prep this afternoon. He couldn't reschedule," Jane said. "So I moved our meeting."

"Without telling me?" I said.

"I'm sure I told you," Jane said. "Besides, you have other priorities."

"I manage my own priorities," I said.

"Not from what I can see," Jane said.

Matty left Deidre and Zibby arranging enormous hats and joined us in the center of the foyer. "Hey El," he said. "You missed a great meeting. Zibby is planning an auction at the Easter Egg Roll. The kids are going to love it."

"I'm sorry I missed it," I said through slightly-gritted teeth and a half-glare to Jane. "You'll have to catch me up. You free for lunch?"

"I can't today," he said and touched Lucy's arm. "Maybe this week, though?"

"Sure," I said.

"You ready?" Matty asked Lucy.

"You two know each other?" I asked. It came out more accusatory than I'd planned.

"Lucy and Kyra were friends in high school," Matty said. "Lucy was in the wedding."

I fought back a look of shock, striving for casual, but I don't think I quite got there. Lucy knew Matty's brother and his wife? Was a bridesmaid at their wedding? I'd known Matty less than three years. Lucy Carmichael knew his whole family?

"Kyra's kept in touch," Lucy said. "Matty, too. Turns out, it's not that hard to do." She tugged on his crisp blue dress shirt and they left.

"Get it together, Elliott," Jane said and turned on her heel, calling out over her shoulder, "So far, I'm not impressed."

Not that I'd agree with her out loud, but I wasn't overly impressed with me either. I felt off my game. Disconnected. I thought of the Ballantynes as my family. More than Edward and Vivi, but the entire Foundation, and by extension, our donors and supporters. Yet I'd let myself drift. I let friendships fade and relationships slide. And my attention to detail had dulled. I hadn't even noticed Jane and Chef were a couple.

I left my messenger bag in my desk drawer and walked to the kitchen, passing the lovely bonnet display in the foyer. Silk flowers and colorful scarves adorned them, one larger than the next.

Carla and Deidre were eating lunch at the steel island in the center of the gigantic kitchen. Double farmhouse sinks graced the far wall beneath a window and copper pots hung from a metal rectangle dangling from the ceiling. I'd say they were mostly decorative, since a beat up stack of pans sat near a twelve-burner stove.

"Carla gave me her recipe for this divine apple chicken

salad," Deidre said. Her gray bob was held away from her face by bright orange readers as she took a bite from a croissant sandwich.

"It's the rosemary pecans," Carla said. "Love is in the details." She handed me a plate with my own sandwich and a pile of her fresh made potato chips. Thin sliced, fried crisp, and so delicious I could eat the entire state of Idaho's worth.

"Jane left you out of the meeting, huh?" Deidre said between bites. Like most of our board members, Deidre was retired. She volunteered at the Sea Pine Library and served on about a dozen committees.

"Yes, and for hardly a reason," I said, feeling defensive. "I'm perfectly capable at managing my time."

"I know, chicken, but this one is close to her," Carla said.

"Did either of you know she was dating Chef Carmichael?" I asked, walking to the wall-length refrigerator freezer to grab a cold Pepsi.

Carla handed me a glass from the wire racking along the far wall. "Nothing definite, but it doesn't surprise me."

"It does me," I said. "Those two fight all the time. They about tore the house down over the setup for the Palm & Fig Ball last December."

"Have you met Jane?" Deidre asked. "She fights with everyone."

"Yeah," Carla added. "It's her way of saying I love you."

"More like her way of breathing," I said through a mouthful of apple chicken salad. When I recovered my manners, I continued. "Did either of you taste Chef's corned beef on Saturday? Or Lola's?"

"I tasted Chef's, briefly," Carla said. "It was surprisingly tasty for his heavy hand, but the same recipe as always."

"I was a judge and judging wasn't to start for another half hour, so I hadn't gotten that far," Deidre said. "Now I'm sorry we didn't start earlier. I would've liked to have tried Lola's cooking." Deidre fumbled with a napkin. "That didn't come out right. I just meant she was a lovely woman, and I didn't spend a minute with her on Saturday. My last chance and I didn't know it."

"None of us did," I said.

"Well, someone knew it," Carla said. "And that someone might just have been Chef Carmichael."

SEVEN

(Day #3: Monday Afternoon)

After Carla shooed us from the kitchen, I grabbed my bag from my office. With the afternoon suddenly free, I needed to get on the road. Time I paid my respects to Chef's mother and Lucy's grandmother, Virginia Carmichael.

Savannah, Georgia was a thirty-minute drive from Sea Pine Island. I took the alternate back route, avoiding the busy highway in favor of a rolling road cut through enormous pines and oaks dripping in Spanish moss. The warm afternoon wind flowed over me as I sped over the asphalt. Once over the Talmadge Memorial Bridge, historic Savannah with its ghostly stories and statued cemeteries enveloped me. Its pace languid, its manner genteel.

Virginia Carmichael lived in an aging part of Savannah. It said old money, but the old in this case meant she had money a long time ago and never multiplied that money to keep up with the Joneses. Or more likely the Hattings, if I were to guess where some of the resentment toward Jane came from. Because Virginia Carmichael could not stand Jane Walcott Hatting.

Though time moved slower in the South, gossip did not. It moved faster than the tide changed directions. And on Sea Pine, that tide changed its mind every twelve hours. Tales of Virginia and Jane's knock-down, drag-outs over historical committee agenda items frequently drifted our way.

I parked in front of a faded yellow Victorian home with grimy white gingerbread trim. It was wedged between its neighbors with a slim strip of land separating them. I climbed the wide steps and rapped on the door.

A woman in a flowered button-down layered with a sturdy vest opened it without a greeting. Her small eyes narrowed as she once-overed my slightly dusty linen ensemble.

"Mrs. Carmichael?" I asked.

"Hmmm-mm."

"I'm Elliott Lisbon with the Ballan—"

"I know who you are. Why're you darkening my doorstep?"

So much for genteel, I thought, and obliged a smile. One caught between friendly and forced. "I'm here to offer my condolences. Mine and the Ballantyne's."

"Condolences?"

"On the loss of your former daughter-in-law, and the, um, well..." My voice drifted as I grappled for the right term. Offering condolences for one's son's arrest did not sound like a time-honored tradition. "And Chef."

"You mean Tom?"

"Yes, of course, Tom. He's been like family to us."

"News to me."

We stood on the porch: me facing the front door, her blocking it.

"Chef Carmichael, Tom, has been involved with many of our events, as a supporter and a contributor."

"Sounds like the same thing."

It kind of did. I resisted the urge to shuffle from foot to foot. I doubted I'd ever called Chef by his given name. Perhaps another reason I felt disconnected. Though in my defense, I did know his name was Tom. "We find it impossible to believe Tom harmed Lola."

"That it?"

"We're here if you need anything. For you and Tom and Lucy. And of course, your other son, Jessie. He wouldn't happen to be here? I'd like to offer my condolences personally."

"Nope."

The high Savannah sun warmed my backside as I tried to find an opening. "I've never actually met Jessie, though I hear he's been very supportive of his brother. Attending our Irish Spring party every year."

"Jessie's a good boy."

"I imagine he is. Tom is good to protect him."

Her gaze narrowed until I could no longer see her eyeballs. "Protect him from what?"

"We seem to have gotten off on the wrong foot. I meant no disrespect, Mrs. Carmichael. I'm only trying to help Chef. Tom. Chef Tom."

"Tom don't need any help. He says he did it, then he did it. Never needed me to fight his battles."

"And Jessie? Does he need Tom to fight his battles?"

"Lucy knows what she's doing. More than you do, I'd wager. We should leave it to her."

"Of course. But I'd like to talk to Jessie. If you happen to know where I can find him..." I casually looked over her shoulder, trying to glimpse inside the house.

She closed the door another inch. "I'd imagine he's on his way to DC by now," she said. "Cherry blossoms in the spring."

"Oh?"

"My Jessie knows how to make the most of the country."

A paneled station wagon creaked up to the low brick curb, barely missing my Mini's bumper. The wagon sludged forward, then back, negotiating its way into the vacancy.

"You 'bout done?" Virginia Carmichael asked. "I'm expecting visitors. Been a hard day."

"I'm really sorry about Tom," I said. "And Lola."

Two women ambled up the short walk, each carrying a glass dish covered in tin foil. Their faces etched with hard lines, their open stares no softer.

I nodded at them and made my leave.

Virginia Carmichael watched me from the porch as I put the Mini in drive and eased on down the road. I cruised her neighborhood, taking three long turns, stopping once to put the top up and grab supplies from my trunk. A pair of binoculars and a box of fruit chews. Standard issue PI-in-training equipment. Tucked inside the Mini, I drove back down Virginia's crowded house-lined street, parking seven doors down from hers.

That Savannah sunshine kept the air a lovely eighty-two degrees. Outside the car, where a breeze and a patch of shade made you want to stroll the streets for an entire afternoon. Inside the car, where one needed to keep the windows rolled up and the engine off for surveillance purposes, it was slightly less strollable. More like stuffy and stifling and oppressive as I kept my head ducked down and watched cranky-looking women lump up Virginia's steps and into her house. For three hours. Some left, but most stayed. The crowd seemed more *Duck Dynasty* than Savannah society. But perhaps all grieving situations required a covered casserole.

I decided to peek in the windows and find out. Easier said than done since the house was situated about ten feet from the curb. Hard to sneak a peek at a full house in broad daylight.

Once foot traffic slowed to zero for fifteen minutes straight, I risked it. Tucking my hair into a floppy hat, I grabbed a canvas beach bag from my backseat and slipped out of the car. I walked with purpose to the house two doors down from Virginia's, then up a side yard no wider than the span of my arms. If I didn't outstretch them at all.

The house's windows were up tall. The sills a solid foot above my head. It allowed me to sneak around to the rear yard without being seen. A narrow alley ran behind the length of this particular row of houses. I kept my head turned away from the back windows and quick-walked to Virginia's yellow Victorian. The house on the south side faced Virginia's directly, nary a rose bush or picket fence to block me from view.

Voices drifted from the open windows across Virginia's back porch as I rounded her house. No one was outside, but ashtrays and half-full glasses of iced tea sat on a side table.

I crept around to the far side of Virginia's house. The neighbor's house to the north was half-blocked by giant hydrangea bushes. An entire row stretched from the alley gate to the front curb. Large green leaves floated on light stems as I inched my way through the thatch.

Luckily, these windows had sills so I could grip and climb. Unluckily, I didn't have the upper body strength to actually pull myself up three feet from the ground. Not without making a lot of noise as I used the house for leverage. Voices continued to ebb and flow through the window screens, but not with enough distinction for me to determine topics or sentences or who was saying what to whom.

Toward the front porch, a side window was slightly lower. I stuffed my hat in my bag and set it next to the house. Balancing one foot on the porch edge, I could lift, pull, and hoist my head over the sill to see through the fluttering curtains. Two women on a sofa. Three others in slat-backed kitchen chairs. One woman leaning in a doorway. I squinted and held my breath. Lucy Carmichael? I popped down before she could spot me and quietly dusted sill grit off my hands. When did she get there? Probably whilst I was lurking around the house. Unless she'd been there the whole time. But she had lunch with Matty and he had the interview at Sea Pine Prep. Not that I kept track of his schedule. It was clearly part of a public conversation.

I snuck back to the Mini and thought about Lucy in the living room. Standing over to the side, her posture more observing than participating. The whole dynamic seemed off. A strange atmosphere, more like a mob meeting. And why so many ladies to comfort Virginia? It was her ex-daughter-in-law who died. Or was the condolence meeting over her son's arrest? Were they circling the proverbial wagons?

My car was right where I left it. Except Nick Ransom was now leaning against the passenger door. Sharply dressed, smelling of sandalwood and ginger, carefully eyeballing me. "Cat burglar or trespasser?" he asked.

"I'm just here offering my condolences," I said. "What about you? Investigator or stalker?"

"I'm just here offering my condolences," he said.

"Uh-huh," I said. "You still believe Chef Carmichael's guilty?"

"Of course."

"Sure, sure. That's why you're here."

Silence followed. I stood on the bumpy brick walk, he leaned on my car.

"What's going on, Ransom? How can you possibly believe Chef killed Lola? Especially like that. So violently and at the Big House."

"It's complicated," he said. "Let me take care of this."

"Why does everyone keep saying that to me? I'm perfectly capable of assisting this investigation. Yours and Lucy's."

"Lucy's?"

"Don't play dumb. I know you know she's here and investigating her own mother's death. How can she not?"

He stood stoic.

"Were there any witnesses at the Irish Spring? Did someone see something? Anything?"

He exuded the austere fortitude befitting a long-suffering Englishman.

"You can help a girl out, Nick Ransom," I said. "Clearly I'm working on this. I'd rather not spend four days interviewing two hundred people to find out no one saw anything."

"Isn't that how you learn? Earn those PI hours legitimately?"

"Don't tease me."

"Who's teasing?"

"I cannot believe for one minute, one second, you have witnesses from the party."

"Why is that?"

"Because it's Monday, a full two days since it happened. I'd have heard all about who saw what and whom from ten different sources by now." I stepped closer to him. "But I'm asking you. To help me. We share, remember?" I knew that witnesses were in the eye of the interviewer. Any minute tidbit might be the key to the whole puzzle, but why double the workload? I trusted Ransom. He was an excellent investigator and the smartest man I'd ever met. Not that I was going to gush that all over him. Or that he needed me to.

"No witnesses," he finally said. "So far."

I waited.

"No one saw Chef with Lola walking toward the Zen garden, and obviously they were there."

He didn't sound surprised at the lack of witnesses, and I wasn't either. The opening bell at the Irish Spring had just rung. Partygoers streamed in full of high excitement. The band was playing, the restaurants set up in every direction. People wouldn't notice things. They'd head straight for the pots of corned beef and cabbage with bread bowls and spring rolls. Who cared who was walking in the garden?

Good news: It saved me tons of time interviewing dozens of

Ballantyne supporters. Bad news: It gave me no new angles or clues or ideas or threads to pull.

Ransom touched my hand, slowly rubbing my fingers. "Hey, you still with me?"

"Yeah, just thinking about the party."

"Did you enjoy the corned beef at the cook-off? You once said you taste-test before the opening bell. Did you get a chance to taste any of the pots?"

My radar started pinging. Faintly, but pinging. "Why do you want to know? It's the recipe, right?"

Before he could answer, a teenager walking seven dogs barreled down the walk. Perhaps the dogs were walking her. They pulled and scurried and barked their little dog heads off when they saw us. "Sorry," she said. "Nearly time for d-i-n-n-e-r."

"Oh crap, I've got pugs!"

"You've got what?" Ransom asked.

"Colonel Mustard and Mrs. White. Pugs. Puppies. They must be starving. Or not. I have no idea when those two eat, but I really should go." I was torn. I wanted to stay and eavesdrop, but I needed to get home. It was strangely nerve-wracking to be responsible for two little creatures who were alone all day without anyone to care for them.

Ransom kissed my forehead, then walked toward Virginia's house. I hopped into the Mini and sped my way through Savannah, over the bridge, through Summerton, over the bridge, through Sea Pine Island, across the gate, and home to my cottage in twenty-seven minutes. I screeched into my drive shortly before seven p.m.

The open living room and kitchen made up the bottom floor of my cottage, while two small master suites made up the top floor. Before I'd left that morning, I'd penned in the pugs to the guest bedroom using the pet carrier as a makeshift roadblock. It was easy enough to do with dogs who are only five inches tall. I peeked through the open door. They were huddled together in the middle of a chewed up set of vintage Mickey Mouse bookends. The wood looked as if it'd been gnawed off by alligators. Tiny Mickey parts were scattered on the carpet.

I rushed over the pet carrier in a panic, convinced the puppies were dead from choking on Mickey's tiny glove hands or one of his yellow shoes. I kicked the edge of one of the bookends and Colonel Mustard startled awake, barking at me before his eyes even opened. Mrs. White joined in and they attacked with the full force of their three-pound pugness.

After a sufficient round of belly rubbing, I gathered up the Mickey parts. A single shoe was missing and a corner of one bookend had been chewed within an inch of its life. I considered it protein and took them down to the kitchen.

They snorfled up dinner as I dined on cereal, our new routine in place. We took a short walk on the beach. They came up to my ankles, so I wasn't too worried about the seasonal dog restrictions. Every human loved those love pugs. They could get away with anything.

We sat on the patio as the evening light faded, leaving the sky streaked with dark orangey clouds. They chewed on regulation Bully Sticks and I finished up my day's notes: Chas, Bitsy, Virginia.

I knew I was too close to things. I couldn't tell the odd details from the normal details. Like Bitsy Obermeyer's car at Tug's on Saturday morning hours before the Irish Spring party. Was it out of place? Why at Tug's when they were closed? Did it even matter?

Or this weird ladies' lunch at Virginia's involving baked foods in glass dishes which no one ate. Oh how I wanted to know what was on the agenda. A conspiracy centered on a murder or a meeting to discuss the latest issue of *Garden &*

Gun? I wondered how I could ask Lucy. Or if I even should. She'd probably not be as forthcoming as I'd like. Or at all.

I made a short list of things I needed to do on Tuesday. My number one priority remained Lola's mortgage and who paid off the balance. My bank visit garnered nothing new. An anonymous benefactor. Could be anyone. Well, anyone willing to spend three hundred eighty-seven thousand dollars on someone else's mortgage and not tell them. I made a note: Why not tell Lola?

My number two priority: Find Jessie Carmichael.

EIGHT

(Day #4: Tuesday Morning)

Drive around any plantation on Sea Pine Island early on a weekday morning and you'll see a fleet of landscape trucks, housekeeping vans, and semi-official security cars roaming the tree-lined streets. Women in tennis whites and men in golf plaid zipped around in electric carts to meet friends for leisurely morning rounds. Young families with colorful towels and lunch baskets walked paths to beaches. Sprinklers watered lawns, fountains decorated ponds.

Not even close to what went on at a trailer park on that same morning. No automatic sprinklers. Women in homemade halters watered their half-lawns with plastic hoses. Men in worn tees climbed into dented beaters to find odd jobs at pawn parlors. Young families crammed into old cars, rushing off to day care, trying to eke out a living.

I cruised the Mini up and down the five rows of Fisher's Landing Trailer Park and Yacht Club. Jessie's spot was vacant. No Winnebago parked or driving or anywhere on the property. Neither was it in Tug's lot. Not the new sailing club across the street, not anywhere along the private road down to the sand. I reluctantly left Washburn Lane and scouted every public beach from the bridge down to Harborside Plantation. I checked shopping centers, strip centers, and even community centers. No Winnebago. I must have driven the full length of Cabana Boulevard, both ways, four times.

It was the fifth time that I spotted it at Captain Blackbeard's Mini Golf. Its painted gold W stuck out from behind a row of bushes. It was tucked into one of the far spots at the rear end of the lot. I parked on its far side, so the Winnebago would block the Mini from view. I walked around the side and knocked on the door. It rattled as if I'd pounded on it with all my might. I peeked in the plastic window, but couldn't see much. Every window was covered in droopy drapes. I pressed my ear against the door. No sounds, just distant traffic whizzing by and laughter wafting through the thick trees from the various holes of mini-golf.

The silver door handle was flat, not a lever or a knob, and opened like a buckle on an airplane seatbelt. I pulled it, but the door remained closed. No deadbolt, just a tiny lock no more complicated than one on an eight-year-old's diary. With two quick twists from a set of pins I carried in my bag, I popped the lock and ducked inside.

My second breaking and entering in twenty-four hours. Definitely not in the regulation PI handbook.

I searched the camper from back to front. First the bedroom area, then the kitchen. Took me all of three glances to realize something wasn't right. Plastic trucks, mismatched dolls, broken crayons littered every flat surface. Dirty plates in the sink indicated a jolly breakfast of chocolate chip pancakes with sticky syrup and greasy bacon for four.

Up front, the gold upholstered captain's chairs swung around when I squeezed past the center console to reach the dash. The glove box snapped open with a push of a button. The registration papers were made out to a Wilbur Radtzel. Beneath the stack: a picture of what could only be grandparents and grandkids in front of a Winnebago. The one I was currently ransacking, I guessed. I carefully returned the paperwork.

My hand was six inches from flinging open the door when I heard voices approach. Muffled and giggling, heading my way. I stepped back three large steps, running into the sidewall where the kitchen met the bathroom. There was no reasonable explanation for me to be inside their family vacation home.

No escape out the front. My closest option was a window directly to my right. It slid open like one in a Barbie camper. No locks, no screen. I sucked in my stomach and didn't breathe and wriggled through that opening faster than a rabbit through a fence. Face first, hands down. My toes caught on the window edge. I did a handstand for one second and thanked the good Lord I wasn't shorter or I would've cracked my skull wide open.

My legs flopped to the side and I scrambled up on tippy toes. I slid the window closed just as the Winnebago shook. The family opened their door and I practically dove into the Mini.

I rested my head on the steering wheel to calm my racing heart and swashed hand-sani across my palms. They stung. The gritty ground cut the soft skin of my hands when I did my acrobatics. I vowed to never ever break in anywhere again. Unless it was an emergency. Only for very important cases. Or I was sure I needed to see what was inside.

Once my heartrate restored itself to a normal rhythm, I chugged the Mini out of the mini-golf lot heading north toward the bridge. I turned off before I reached it. I cruised three miles along the sound on Old Pickett Road until I pulled into the Wharf.

Sprawling oaks hid most of the restaurant from the parking area. Inside, patrons were greeted with sweeping views of the Palmetto Bridge while they dined on French-fusion cuisine on fine china plates at white-clothed tables.

It was only late morning, the Wharf wouldn't open until

late afternoon, but I'd hoped to talk to someone on staff. I didn't recognize the servers dressing the main dining room, so I showed myself to the kitchen. Through the swinging door, a flurry of cooks chopped and stirred and peeled and prepped. I still didn't recognize anyone. Seemed as if Chef Carmichael had hired quite a few new staff members since I'd been there last. Which was when I was in the middle of another murder investigation. I wondered if that had helped or hurt his dinner business. They said bad press was still good press. I thought about Tate Keating and his recent headline about Lola and the Ballantyne. Sometimes bad press was bad press.

A young woman in a white chef's coat exited an enormous steel door carrying a tray of trussed hens. Or quails. Or some kind of something. "Elliott?"

"Hey," I said. "Julie, right?"

"Julia," she said and set the tray down. "What brings you by?" Before I could answer, she held up her finger, likely just figuring out exactly what brought me by. She said something to another cook and grabbed a towel. "Let's talk in the dining room."

I followed her to a four-top next to a large picture window overlooking the bridge. Water from the sound lapped against wide trunks of tree, its leaves floating in the soft waves.

"This is about Chef, right?" She wrapped her hands in the towel. First drying them, then wringing them.

"It is, but how are you? It's nice to see you. Looks like you got a promotion." I nodded at the words embroidered on her coat.

She smiled and touched her new title spelled out in blue thread. "I did. Sous chef. After last December's cook-off fiasco..." her voice drifted off.

Zibby Archibald's niece had trained here at the restaurant and calling it a fiasco was apropos. Another connection between the Ballantyne and the Wharf. And now Chef and Lola and even Jane.

"Did you go to the Irish Spring?" I asked.

"I did. My first as sous," she said. "We set up early. The team finished prepping and was ready for service about five minutes before the opening bell."

"I hate to ask, but how was Chef acting? Worried, stressed, angry?"

"Not any of those things. He was happy, really," she said. "Well, you know, not happy like a normal person is happy. He yelled at three servers and freaked out over the diced onions, which were more chopped than diced, but that's happy for him."

"Jessie, his brother, was there?"

"Yeah, but I don't know him. He wasn't really around us that much. He ate the bread we kept slicing. Dipped it right into the stock pot like a caveman."

"Did he seem angry or stressed?"

"I don't know. We were pretty busy. He just seemed underfoot. Especially with Chef." She started wringing the towel again.

"What is it? I'm only here to help Chef, I promise. You know how important he is, how important you all are, to the Ballantyne."

"I know, I know," she said. "Okay, well, it seemed like his brother was goading Chef. Trying to get under his skin. I was on the other side of the table. I couldn't hear what they were saying. It's only an impression, so I could be way off."

"Every little bit helps," I said and patted her twisty hands. "What about his mother, Virginia? Was she there?"

"I doubt it. But I wouldn't recognize her. I've never met her."

"Not even here at the Wharf?"

"She's never eaten here."

"How long have you worked for Chef?"

"Over two years, but it's legend. His mother has never once crossed that entrance. I doubt she was at the Irish Spring."

A server in a waist apron placed water goblets across the room. The light clinking of glasses against the table mixed with the sounds of pots banging from the nearby kitchen.

"What can you tell me about Chef's recipe for the contest? His winning corned beef and cabbage."

"He usually only makes it for your party," she said. "He's only made it here once or twice. Special occasions, that kind of thing. It's pretty amazing. I don't know why he doesn't make it more often. It's the best you'll ever taste."

"I think Lola may have used his recipe on Saturday to enter the contest."

"It's the other way around. Chef used Lola's recipe. He always did." She folded the cloth towel. "Rumor has it, anyway."

"How solid is this rumor?"

"More of an open secret."

Chef Carmichael won the Ballantyne's Pot of Gold contest every year with Lola's recipe? Only slightly arrogant of him to personally autograph the cookbook to the person whose recipe he stole.

Maybe Lola threatened him. She'd tell everyone it wasn't his recipe, it was hers. And Chef's reputation meant more to him than her life. Maybe he really did kill her. She went to the Irish Spring with the same recipe, her recipe, to show off. Could Ransom actually think that?

"Did you see Lola with Chef? Or anyone around the Zen garden?" I asked.

"I didn't even know there was a Zen garden," Julia said.

"It's by the steps to the pool," I said. "There are water lily topiaries and a rock sculpture at the entrance."

"Yeah, I know where it is now."

"Right, sorry," I said.

"I didn't see anyone. My head was down most of the time. Filling bowls and slicing bread."

"When did Chef leave the booth?"

"Maybe fifteen minutes before the bell. Not much before that."

"Was Jessie at the booth when Chef left?"

"No, they were both gone," Julia said. "I remember because it was peaceful. They'd stopped arguing, and we got twice as much done."

"What were they arguing about? Even a snippet is useful."

She twisted her towel. I could almost see her weighing her answer, if it would help Chef or hurt him. "Money, maybe."

"Did Jessie owe Chef money?"

"Actually, it was more that Jessie wanted his money or something about what Chef owed him. They were yelling, but whispering. You know, trying to be quiet but not doing a good job of it. I didn't want to eavesdrop and was glad they stepped away."

"Thank you, Julia, I know this is hard."

"It haunts me. That moment of relief when Chef left the booth. If only he hadn't. I almost called out to him. We needed the help, but I was so happy the bickering stopped, I just let him go. What if I had called out and kept him at the station? None of this would've happened."

I looked at her, meeting her sad eyes. "Maybe not none of it. But at least Chef would be in the kitchen, not in the jail."

"What happens if Chef goes to prison?" Julia asked.

She stood and I followed.

"I don't know," I said and pushed the chair against the table, then righted the white china plate in front of it.

"His biggest rival, Chef Newhouse, came in last night," she said. "Dined right at this table."

"Word travels fast." As did reputations.

"I think he was scoping us out," she said. "Like he wanted to buy Chef's restaurant. Or worse."

"Worse?"

"Take it from him."

NINE

(Day #4: Tuesday Afternoon)

With a heavy soul, I returned to my cottage. I took the pugs for a quick walk along the shore. They ran on the hardpacked sand while salty water washed over their paws. Like toddlers, they dashed toward the water, then quickly away when it touched them. After I toweled them dry, I carried them upstairs. One squirmy pug in each hand. The stairs could sometimes be a challenge, and as much as I wanted to spend a slow hour watching them conquer my staircase, I had someplace to be.

We sat together on the floor of my closet. They attempted to chew my flip flops while I debated my wardrobe. It was St. Patrick's Day. The day of Lola's wake. I wanted to wear black from head to toe, hat to shoe. Heavy, dark, mournful black. The color of sorrow. But Lola was vibrant and sparkly and the color of life. I didn't know how to balance those aspects. My sorrow at the loss of her life. Her life in need of honoring.

The lucky green frock I'd worn at the party, spotted with Lola's blood, now lay at the bottom of the trash bin out by the street. I only owned one other green ensemble, the one I took to the party as my option B. It still hung in its garment bag in my office. I couldn't bring myself to go get it. To dress in a dress I almost wore on the last day of her life.

I went with black.

Tug Boat Slim's was packed. Cars jammed the lot, the street, and down to the waterway. People lined the slatted walk to the front and spilled onto the deck out back. I wiggled my way inside, scooching past dozens of patrons, nearly all holding frosty hurricane glasses filled with festive red drinks adored with fresh pineapple wedges. Singapore Slings.

Tug Jensen lined up a row of glasses along the front of the bar. Bottles of gin and cherry brandy mingled with bowls of pineapples and lime. He lifted a glass to me with sad eyes and a pained smile. He looked as heartbroken as I felt. I needed to ask him about Lola. How close they were, how this could happen. But not here. Not now.

"Hey Elliott," he said, handing me a Singapore Sling. "Thanks for coming."

"Of course." I raised my glass in toast to Lola Carmichael, Tug did the same. I sipped, he drank, and the crowd swelled behind me.

"How are Colonel Mustard and Mrs. White?" he asked over the loud rumble of voices. "Lola adored them. Called 'em her babies."

"I adore them, and Vivi will, too," I said.

He nodded toward the back of the room where Lucy sat. "I don't think she could've handled taking care of them right now. You're kind to do so. Makes it a little easier."

I nodded, but wasn't sure I agreed. Nothing would make it easier for her. I lost both of my parents when I was about ten years younger than she was now. It was unbelievably difficult and I hadn't been as close to my mom as she was to hers.

Tug continued making Slings and I pushed my way through the throng to Lucy in the far corner. I waved to her and she waved back. It startled me to realize I felt relief. I'd wondered if she'd welcome my company or reject it.

"I'm sorry, Lucy," I said when I reached her and hugged her

tight. "I'm so so sorry." She nodded against my shoulder, then pulled back. "You're alone?" I asked.

"Yeah, I don't think anyone knows what to say to me," she said as we sat. "But Matty'll be by later."

I resisted asking about Matty. I wanted to, but silently questioned why I wanted to know. We'd stopped dating months ago at my urging. He was a best friend to me, someone I leaned on and loved, but not in the way one loves when dating. I made that decision, the right decision. Yet here I sat, a sharp pang at the thought of him dating someone else. Someone I called a friend. Or used to.

"What about Virginia or Jessie?" I asked.

"They're at the parade in Savannah. Second largest in the nation."

"Is that why you held the wake today?"

She tipped her drink at me. "Two birds, one St. Patrick's Day."

"When is the funeral?" I raised my voice to be heard over the crowd and winced. It didn't seem appropriate to shout about a funeral.

"This is it," she said with a sloppy wave around the room. That was quite possibly not her first Singapore Sling of the afternoon. "Harry's done with the autopsy. Nothing unusual. Other than she died." She took a long sip from her straw. "You know, I came down here over Christmas two Christmases ago. It's been awhile."

"I'm sorry, Lucy, I don't know—"

"Remember when we played cribbage at mom's until two in the morning? And those kids tried to scam the pinball machines in the game room? She broke it up and tracked them down, each and every one."

"Made them return every penny. And it was like hundreds of pennies, right?"

Lucy laughed. "Yeah. Like five bucks or something. She chased them with a tennis racket or lacrosse stick?"

"It was a fishing pole."

"Right, right. The fishing pole," Lucy said. "Used it like a whip. Taught them they couldn't steal from her."

"Remember the year she oversold the RV spots and they were lined up down the road?"

"She sold spots to the overgrown woods across the street. Told them it was the nature package." Lucy stirred her drink, then took a pull from the straw. "Guess the new development gets in the way now."

"Do you know much about it? Was Lola interested in it?"

"Is that why you showed up?" Her drink splashed when she thumped it on the table. "You're not here for me. You don't want to relive the good old days. You want to question me? Well, back off, Elliott. I got this."

I reached out to touch her hand, but she pulled away. "Lucy, I'm here for you."

"Where have you been? I started school and you just disappeared. When I left town, I guess I just left your life."

"I'm so sorry," I said. It sounded lame and inadequate. "I screwed up." I paused and leaned against the chair to put some space between us. I didn't know how to continue without making this all about me. Tonight was all about Lucy and Lola. "I'm grateful we spent so much time together. And I'm grateful I knew your mother. She was sassy and bold and kind."

Lucy nodded and stared into her drink. I looked away, trying not to intrude. Imogene, Lola's friend, walked into Tug's, her son, Austin, by her side. Imogene waved at me and elbowed him and tried to make her way over, bumping past Chas and Bitsy Obermeyer. They awkwardly held a pair of Singapore Slings. Even Julia from the Wharf was there talking to Tug. All this sadness crammed into one room. No good reason this happened to Lola or to lose her so soon.

"I know you've got this," I said. "But this is one case you shouldn't work by yourself. It's too much, Lucy. Let me help."

"I said I got this."

"I'm actually really good at this."

"So am I."

"I found out something today that might be useful. Did you know Chef used Lola's recipe for the cook-off? The one he's won like seven times and used in his own bestselling cookbook?"

"He had Lola's permission. He even credits her in the acknowledgements. Read the whole book."

"That doesn't—"

"I mean it," Lucy said. "I got this. One more day, two tops, and I can wrap it up. A couple of calls, one more stop. I've been shaking the trees and something big is about to fall out." She downed the rest of her Sling and stood. "Fastest I've ever closed a case. Mom would be proud."

Lucy left me at the table, slipping out the side door. I watched Matty walk up the path as she walked down it. He leaned down and kissed her. They hugged. They talked. They turned away from Tug's and disappeared into the early evening.

I saw Imogene and her son wedging their way toward me and I wasn't up for it. With a final sip of my own Sling, I followed Lucy's path and snuck out the door and into the early evening.

I turned on a single lamp in my living room. Lola's cookbook on my driftwood coffee table, both pugs on the sofa next to me. Soft sounds of the surf against the sand floated through the screen of the open slider.

I knew I should feel motivated. Energized to track down whoever took Lola Carmichael's life. Stole it right in front of me and God and everyone at the Big House. A place I felt safe. A place I thought Lola would be safe. Where everyone would be safe.

But I didn't feel motivated. I felt heavy and blue and wanted to sit on my sofa forever.

Sid knocked on my front door before letting herself in. She carried two enormous totes that nearly weighed her down, and that's saying something. Sid was built like a professional volleyball player: tan, tall, and could take down just about anyone with a single spike of her fist.

"*Alias* or *Grey's*?" she asked, dumping the bags on the table. "You want to kick some ass or cry your eyes out?"

"Cry my eyes out."

Colonel Mustard and Mrs. White leapt from the cushions like Mighty Mouse and Co., skidding to a stop at Sid's flip-flopped feet. "Well, aren't you two the cutest things since Kate Spade handbags became a thing."

I riffled through one of the totes, flipping through DVDs, setting aside all five seasons of *Alias* in favor of the *Grey's Anatomy* discs. I wanted moving melodrama set to a heart-wrenching musical backdrop. "This one," I said and popped open the cover. "Season two."

"Ah, *Into You Like a Train*?"

"Right," I said. "Life doesn't get more helplessly sorrowful than that."

Sid opened two bags of Popcorn Indiana: my favorite Kettlecorn, her favorite Movie Theatre, while I tossed down two Bullies for the pugs.

"What are those things?" Sid asked.

"Some kind of beef flavored chew stick," I said. "Like cat nip for dogs. Dog nip."

Sid and I sat end to end on my sofa, draped in the afghan Vivi Ballantyne crocheted for me when I was in the third grade.

We watched Meredith and Derek and Christina and George juggle medicine and love for five episodes until the sixth when a train wreck ruined everything and Meredith watched and screamed and cried and couldn't stop it. I cried with her, then fell into a sorrowful state of misty blue.

At close to midnight, Sid left me weepy under the afghan after I insisted she leave. I had Colonel Mustard and Mrs. White and an entire box of Double Stuf Oreos. I'd make it through the night on my own.

I'd just drifted to sleep when my phone beeped. With swollen eyes, I read the text. Ransom. *I'm coming over.*

I texted back. *I'm okay. Just need to rest.*

Thirty seconds later my front doorbell rang. The pugs went crazy as if the cottage was being invaded by a crew of burglaring cats. They barked so hard, their bodies bounced as they raced to the front door.

I dragged the afghan behind me and cracked open the door. My eyes burned in the glow of the porch light and Ransom slipped inside.

"Hey there," he said. First a kiss on my cheek, then he knelt to rub two pairs of soft puppy ears. "You must be the starving pugs."

They licked his hands between barks and bounces.

Ransom stood and put his hands on my shoulders. "Lucy's at Island Memorial Hospital."

I tried to shake the sleep from my foggy brain. "Why? Did she find something?"

"She was shot. At Lola's."

"Shot? At Lola's?"

"I thought you'd want to know."

"Is she okay? She must be. Shot isn't dead, right?" I balled up the quilt and threw it on the sofa.

"She's out of surgery, Red. But it's touch and go."

"Surgery? She's out already? What took you so long to tell me?"

"The two uniforms called to the scene didn't connect her to Lola at the Big House. But a doctor eventually did when she was in recovery." He kissed my forehead, then opened the door. "I told you as soon as I knew, I promise. I'm headed out. I'm meeting the team at Lola's. I'll call you later."

"Thanks," I said, my mind racing. "I'll be at the hospital."

TEN

(Day #5: Wednesday Early Morning)

Within thirty minutes, I parked the Mini in the quiet lot at Island Memorial Hospital and raced through the large automatic doors. I didn't stop to ask which room Lucy was in. I simply fast-walked past the welcome desk, through emergency, to the white board where every emergent patient's name was written in sloppy black marker. I found CARMICHAEL, L three names from the bottom. Room 317.

That was a good sign, I thought to myself as I punched the up button on the elevator one dozen times. The third floor meant she was in a regular room. Possibly ICU. At least it was a room with a bed, not a surgery table.

I continued to walk with purpose, slowing only to help myself to a squirt of hand-sani from the canisters mounted to the walls, until I reached her room.

Lucy lay in an oversized twin bed. An IV taped to her hand, the tube dangled from a bag on a hanger. Faint swishing and rhythmic beeped in time with her heartbeat. Bruises covered the left side of her face. Bandages wrapped around her shoulder and upper arm.

"Excuse me," a nurse said in a soft voice. "Are you her family?"

"A family friend," I said. "How is she?"

The nurse touched my arm and guided me toward the door. "I'm sorry, only family may visit."

"Well, then, yes, I'm family. Obviously she's my sister."

"I'm sorry, ma'am, but you need to leave."

"Look, if I'd just said yes the first time you asked, it wouldn't be an issue."

"Lying isn't the answer," she said, giving me a tougher shove toward the door.

"Wait," I said, planting my feet solidly on the rubber tile floor still inside the room. "Lucy doesn't have family here, not really. She lost her mom on Saturday in a terrible, horrible...at my house. Not my house. The Big House—"

"This is Lola's girl?" She grabbed Lucy's chart, a stack of papers on a clipboard, from the wall outside the door.

"You knew Lola?"

"Sure did. From down at Tug's. My daughter's a waitress there on the weekends."

"I'm Elliott Lisbon with the Ballantyne Foundation," I said, pleading with this woman in pale pink scrubs. "I'm as close to family as Lucy has right now." Which was true because I had no idea where Jessie was or how to contact him.

The nurse stuck the clipboard into the slot on the wall and glanced around. "Okay, for an hour max. It'll be nice for her to not be alone."

"Thank you, thank you," I said and squeezed her arm. "How is she? Is she sleeping?"

"She's in a medically-induced coma."

I blanched, feeling my face turn green at the word coma. "What the hell happened?" I blurted out. "She was beaten, shot, had surgery, and is now in a coma, all in a few hours?"

"It's okay. Surgery was minor," the nurse said, her voice still low. "She was shot in the shoulder, and it didn't do too much damage. But she took a blow to the head and her brain had slight swelling. The coma will help her rest."

Lucy lay still. The machines hummed and beeped and swished. The nurse patted my arm. "Now only an hour. About the time when the police corporal will show up to guard her room."

I nodded and went to Lucy's side. I pulled up a chair then pulled out my phone. I texted Sid. *You still awake?*

Obvs. Nightcapping at the Blue Martini. You need me to come back?

Yes, but to the hospital. Lucy was shot and I need a favor.

On my way.

Sid was on the hospital board, which gave her access to places I didn't have.

Lucy's steady breathing kept me reassured while I waited. I watched the clock and the array of machines until Sid walked in shortly after one a.m.

She hugged me tight, then pulled back. "How is she?"

I told her what the nurse told me. "Now we wait."

"I'm here for you, sweetie."

"Where's Milo?" I eyeballed her outfit. A slinky dress and pointy-toed shoes. "Late night booty call?"

"Ha ha. We had a date. Which I delayed because you needed me. I would've stayed with you all night."

"I'm sorry. I know. I'm just cranky and confused and exhausted." I rubbed my hands over my face.

"It's okay. Really. Now what's this favor?"

"Can you find her personal belongings? I want something."

Sid glanced at Lucy, beaten and swollen and in a coma. "A bit opportunistic?" she asked delicately.

"No, not like that. She got too close to something, or someone, likely to do with her mother. I need to find out what it was or who it was and catch them myself."

"Are you too close, too? You could be in danger."

"I don't think so. I'm snuggling pugs and she's shaking trees. She shook a tree and something fell out and shot her. Apparently I'm not even close."

"What do you need?"

"Her stuff. Whatever she had with her when they brought her in. And I need it before Jessie Carmichael, her father, shows up and claims all the stuff as her official kin."

Sid leaned back to look at the nurses' desk. "Official kin? What kind of kin are you?"

"I'm official-ish."

Sid nodded and left the room. A minute later Milo Hickey entered it. He was tall and handsome with dark skin and short dark hair. His suit tailor-made, his shoes handmade.

We hugged and I told him how Lucy was doing.

"I have a banking question on a mortgage," I said softly, foregoing the obvious smack to my head. Another sign I had no game. I never once thought to contact him.

Milo Hickey was the CEO of his own asset management firm, Hickey Thompson Equities. He was sophisticated and smart. He also hosted underground poker games. "The mortgage on your cottage?" he asked.

"No, that's paid in full. A gift from my late parents." I realized the irony, or maybe coincidence, of thinking about the mortgage my late parents left me while standing in front of Lucy, talking about the mortgage her late mother left her. Or left her father. Did that make it better or worse? "I met with Lola last week. She was quite concerned someone paid her late mortgage for her."

"And that's a bad thing?" he said, echoing the same question I'd asked Lola.

"In light of what happened to her, I'd say yes." I stepped closer and lowered my voice. "Lola was really late on the payments. Fisher's Landing was about to go into foreclosure when someone paid the outstanding balance. In full. Anonymously."

"Anonymously is impossible. There's always a record. It's the law."

"I checked with the bank personally. There was no name or ID on the transaction."

"There's always a record," he repeated.

"The head of the bank, any bank, can see exactly who paid it off?"

"Yes. Their information is part of the mortgage record."

"No matter what? Even if it's paid anonymously?" I'm pretty sure Milo held back a significant eye roll. "I'm just being thorough," I added.

"No such thing as anonymous in banking," he said. "There's always a detailed paper trail."

I nodded slowly, hoping the frustration and irritation I felt didn't show up all over my face. Chas Obermeyer refused to give me information, denied its very existence, which Milo claimed was on record. What was Chas up to this time?

Sid walked in and shoved a bedpan between me and Milo, trying to hand it to me.

I gasped. Out loud. "Do you know me?"

"It's fresh from the wrapper. Pinkie swear. I needed something to carry everything in."

I peeked inside. A slim wallet. A set of keys. A pen. A half-full pack of gum. Two receipts. One for gas, one for the gum. No notebook, no phone. I gingerly lifted out the keys. "Thank you. These might help."

With another hug from both Sid and Milo, they left with the bedpan to return Lucy's things to the emergency desk.

I said goodbye to Lucy, then talked with the nurse. "I really appreciate your kindness."

"She's a good girl, and I loved her mother. Everyone did."

She tipped her head toward the oncoming man in a police uniform.

"Thank you," I said. I gave her my card. "If you need anything, please call me."

I went the opposite way down the hall, away from the officer assigned to Lucy's room, her keys clutched in my hand.

Once back in the Mini Coop, I stared at my phone. I needed to call Matty. It was now after two a.m. Certainly he'd be sleeping and certainly he'd want to know.

He answered on the third ring. Groggy, but coherent. "Elliott? What's wrong?"

"Hey Matty. Sorry to wake you. I know it's late, but I thought I should call."

"Sure, El, what's up?"

"It's about Lucy. She was shot tonight. She's at Island Memorial."

"Is she okay? How bad?" His voice faded in and out and muffled sounds thumped in the background. A man on the move.

"She's okay. She's in a medically-induced coma, but the nurse said it was normal. I'm here now. Well, leaving here now."

"What happened? A burglary? At the trailer park?"

"I don't know," I said softly. "I hate to ask, but you were with her tonight—"

"Hey—"

"I didn't mean it like that. I meant, it's just that the police are investigating and you were likely one of the last people to see her. I know she was rattling cages on her mother's case."

"She said she was nearly wrapped up. That's all she'd say. We left the wake, but she really wanted to be left alone. So I gave her space." His tone had changed. Still worried, but now with an added layer of tension both from my questions and from Lucy's dangerous activities.

"What time?" I asked.

"Not late, maybe eight? Anything else? I need to get there."

"That's all, Matty," I said. "I'm sorry."

"Me, too." And with that, he was gone.

I knew being in the middle of an investigation grated on Matty. It had when I was dating him. The invasive questions, the ugly side of humanity, the precarious situations involving said ugly side of humanity.

I slowly drove back to my cottage, the cool night air accompanying me through the empty streets. Wind rustled palm fronds and distant frogs squawked in random beats. I wanted to sit with Lucy at the hospital. Cry in Lola's trailer. Fly to Greenland and hug Vivi and Edward until they made it all better. All was not right in my world and I didn't know what to do.

ELEVEN

(Day #5: Wednesday Morning)

Things were moving fast. Too fast. Lola killed and Lucy shot, all in three days. I needed to think. I needed to shake off the blue. I wasn't the victim. This didn't happen to me. It happened to my friends. They needed me to get it together. I woke up at the crack of six thirteen a.m. and started cleaning. Bathrooms, floors, rugs, linens, laundry. With each spritz, each scrub, I organized thoughts in my brain. Always circling back to the question of: Who would do this? With why coming in a close second. And third: what would happen next?

After the floors gleamed and the countertops sparkled, I turned to the pugs. I decided to give those two firebrands a bath.

Do not try this at home.

Every surface of my kitchen was puddle-soaked as if my cottage was equipped with fire sprinklers and they went off mid-wash.

Took me an additional thirty minutes to clean a kitchen I'd already cleaned. Finally I showered, dressed, and grabbed my bag. With the pugs' carrier blocking the guest room doorway, I waved goodbye. They looked up with their big brown seal eyes, curly tails wagging.

It was still early and I still didn't have a plan. I had determination, but that wasn't actionable.

"We need a bike ride," I told them. "Exercise and endorphins." I'd never actually experienced the endorphin rush athletes raved about, but whatevs. My first stop this morning was the police station and that required a particular strategy. A trip around the neighborhood gave me time to formulate it.

I released the hounds and we ran down the stairs to the garage. They were so much more fearless going down the steps than up. It took only a minute to make a blanket bed in the basket of my bike. They sniffed and inspected, but I didn't think they'd escape. With harnesses in place and the leashes tucked in beside the dogs, we set off from the garage. I'd barely hit my driveway when I realized it was quite sunny out. Did pugs get sunburned? In the morning? With my luck, you bet. I sat in the drive, balanced on my three-wheeler, deciding what to do. I had no bonnets for them, but I did have an umbrella. Do not ask me how I planned to steer the bike whilst holding an umbrella over two excited pugs on a ten-mile-long bike ride around Oyster Cove Plantation.

"Be right back," I said. "I have just the thing."

I ran into the garage and rummaged through the Mini. I found a small umbrella, the kind with a telescoping stem and a one-foot wingspan. I tossed it back. The puppies were small, but not that small.

Having lived at or near the beach for the last twenty years, my garage held many a golf and beach umbrella. In the corner on a top shelf was a jumbo of a canopy. One to provide enough shade for a two-block radius.

"Got it!"

As soon as I said it, I heard a car door slam, then tires squeal.

I walked to my bike and the pugs were gone. An old blue car raced up the road.

"Oh my God!" I screamed. I tossed the umbrella to the side

and ran to the Mini. I screeched out of the driveway and followed the car toward the Oyster Cove exit.

I dialed the gate. "Come on, come on." It rolled to an automatic answering system. "For a guest pass, please press one. For management, please press—" I pressed four for the gatehouse, having heard this recording seven thousand times.

I pressed four and waited. And waited. It was still ringing when I reached the gate. The restrictive bar was open, as it usually was during daytime hours, allowing residents to leave without waiting for the slow bar to rise and fall.

I flew through the opening and speed-dialed Ransom. I hadn't noticed if his silver racer was parked in front of his cottage next to mine. Didn't matter. No answer.

I dialed 911.

The blue car took a right on Cabana without slowing.

"Nine-one-one, what's your emergency?"

"Someone stole my dogs," I said. "They're driving a blue Cadillac Seville. Faded blue. Old blue. I'm too far away to get the license plate."

"Elli Lisbon?" the dispatcher asked.

"Yes, right, caller ID," I said. "I'm traveling north on Cabana, just past Oyster Cove Plantation, toward the bridge."

"Is this like the time you were searching for the missing Pomeranian?"

"No. Yes. No. There are two pugs and someone stole them from my bike basket," I said.

"Your bike basket?"

"Yes," I said. "Just now. Maybe two minutes ago, three, tops. The car is traveling at high speed on Cabana. I'm doing sixty-seven in a stretch of forty and he's racing away from me. Not slowing down for lights, by the way."

Her tone changed. "I'm calling patrol. What is your exact location?"

We were nearing the turn off to The Wharf restaurant. "North on Cabana, about to cross Old Pickett Road."

She kept me on hold while I sped closer to the Cadillac. Traffic was light, but the car was still forced to dart between lanes. I swerved around a minivan in the left lane. Slammed my brakes as the car in the right lane slowed to turn on a side street.

I barely glanced over my shoulder to switch lanes and punched the gas. Taillights blinked ahead as the Cadillac tapped them at a red light. Then blew right through it.

Sirens blared in the distance. Behind me, in front of me.

We were nearing the bridge to mainland South Carolina. Once over, the car might be gone forever. With Lola's pugs. My pugs. Vivi's pugs.

The Cadillac veered hard left to avoid a string of cars parked on the shoulder.

Panic and adrenaline rushed to my head. Were the pugs loose in that car? What if he crashed?

We closed in on the bridge. The car was a hundred feet away. Then eighty. I was getting closer.

A long camper pulled out of Washburn Lane, leisurely turning onto Cabana, dead in front of the Cadillac.

"Oh my God. Oh my God. Oh my God."

The truck part turned long before the camper part. The Cadillac slammed on its brakes. It fishtailed onto Washburn. I skidded my turn behind him, watching the car gain speed as it sprinted down the street. The dead-end street.

Sirens wailed from somewhere behind me. I glanced in the rearview. No police cars. No cars. Just a mile of empty road.

The Cadillac headed down the narrow lane to the beach. Its taillights flashed as it bumped onto the sandy strip.

By the time I reached the lane, the Cadillac was no longer speeding. It had stopped. Its front end wedged between two trees. Its back end jutted into the lane. The driver's door was open, the engine still running.

I skidded to a stop. Flung open my door and ran full out to the Cadillac, scared shitless at what I might find.

Pug barks greeted me through the open window. I climbed into the Cadillac. A crate big enough for a large cat had been buckled into the backseat. Colonel Mustard and Mrs. White were tucked inside on a thick foam pad.

Two minutes later, two police cars with sirens blasting parked behind the Mini. Two minutes is a lifetime when you're waiting for the police and a bad guy has the lead.

"Elliott," Parker said.

I turned around and sat on the edge of the driver's seat. I pointed down the lane toward the beach with a shaking hand. "I didn't see who, but had to have gone that way."

Two patrol officers ran down the beach path.

"What happened?" Parker asked.

"I'm not sure." I put my head between my knees and tried to breathe deeply. My voice cracked and my hands still shook. "I was taking the pugs. I'd put them in my bike basket. Wanted to ride them around the plantation. I've been neglecting them. They needed shade from the sun. I barely grabbed the umbrella. I heard a car door slam. They were gone."

"You didn't see the driver? Male, female?"

"No, nothing." I sat up and got out of the car. "I didn't even try to get the license plate. I just drove."

Parker helped me push the driver's seat back and lift the crate out. Colonel Mustard and Mrs. White still had their harnesses on, their leashes dangled from the carrier onto the car's floor mat.

I let them out. They barked and snapped at my ankles.

Parker leaned down to give them scratches.

"Sorry, Corporal," one of the patrol officers said. "We didn't see anyone in the brush or on the beach."

"He has to be there!" I nearly screamed. "He was just right here."

"Or she," Parker said.

"Right. Or she," I said. "How could they get away so fast?"

"Can you run the plate?" Parker asked one of the officers. He walked to his cruiser and the other stayed with us.

"We split up," he said. "But the bramble is thick and the tide is in. No footprints, no voices, no sounds."

"Car was reported stolen," the first officer hollered over. "Out of Savannah this morning."

"Call in the canine unit from the county," Parker said. "And another patrol unit. Put out a call to watch for foot traffic on the bridge."

I knew this was more about a stolen car and crazy driver who endangered the lives of the Sea Pine citizens than it was about my pugnapped puppies. But it didn't matter. As long as they found whoever did this.

"What's that?" Parker asked. She pointed to a letter-sized envelope stuck in the driver's seat. A booklet of stamps and a pen had fallen to the floor near the brake pedal.

The front was addressed to *Vivienne Ballantine*. It wasn't sealed.

Parker put on evidence gloves and slid out a thin sheet of paper. A short note written in sloppy scrawl. *One million dollars for the return of the dogs. Further instructions will arrive this afternoon.*

No signature, no other marks or words.

"Why Vivi Ballantyne?" Parker said.

"These were her pugs. Lola's originally. She left them to Vivi in her will. I'm taking care of them until Vivi returns from Greenland. Which is Friday."

"Who knew Vivi was the rightful owner and not you?" Parker asked. "It seems like specific information, them staying at your house."

"I don't know who knows. I said something about Vivi to Tug last night at the wake. But there were so many people there." Julia, Chas, Bitsy, Imogene, Austin, half of Sea Pine Island, all of Fisher's Landing. Maybe some of Virginia's *Duck Dynasty* crew? "Lucy and Jessie likely had copies of the will or at least knew about it. Both were in it. But no one knew I was going to take the puppies on a bike ride this morning. I'd just decided. Like ten minutes before I loaded them up." That thought made my knees even weaker. I leaned on the stolen car's bumper. "They were at my house. Waiting. What if I'd left them alone?"

Parker squeezed the mic on the handset attached to the shoulder of her uniform. She relayed the info and my address to dispatch. "We'll get someone over there right now," she said.

"You said this car was stolen out of Savannah?" I asked.

"Yep, this morning."

"The Carmichael clan lives in Savannah," I said. "And was also privy to Lola's will."

"I'll tell the lieutenant."

"Thank you." I gently returned the pugs to the crate and together Parker and I put them in my car. "You'll keep me posted?"

"Definitely."

I talked to the pugs the entire drive back to my cottage. Soothing them and me. By the time we'd returned home, a patrol car out front, my bike in the driveway, my garage door wide open, I'd vowed to find who tried to take them and promised to keep them safe.

I hoped I wouldn't break that promise.

TWELVE

(Day #5: Wednesday Morning)

The officer assured me all was safe at my house. He checked all points of entry and together we inspected every closet and cupboard. I started to leave Colonel Mustard and Mrs. White upstairs, but I couldn't leave them unguarded. I debated for five minutes standing in the doorway, and I knew I couldn't leave them alone all day. Or ever alone by themselves. I was still shaky and panicky and out of sorts. My thoughts were jumbly which set my very mild OCD on edge. Like the very sharp edge of a very tall cliff over a very deep canyon.

After triple checking every door and window lock, I gathered the pugs into their own carrier and tucked them into the backseat of the Mini. Driving with the vigilance reserved for getaway drivers, repeatedly checking my rearview, jumping every time a car switched lanes behind me, I eventually eased my way over the Palmetto Bay bridge and into Summerton. Destination: Happy Tails.

I'd never actually been to any pet shop, whether warehouse or family owned, but I'd seen this one many times traveling to and from the island, zooming past its natural wood structure and quippy sayings on the changeable letter signs by the road. *It's all fun and games until someone ends up in a cone. We love all animals and most people. Pets welcome, children must be leashed.*

"You're going to be fine," I said aloud. To them or me, I wasn't sure it mattered.

We walked inside, the carrier clutched to my chest, my steps slow and steady.

"Whatcha got there?" a nice lady in an apron asked. If ever a woman looked like a storybook grandma, she did. One with a hot pink streak in her hair and weird Birkenstock-like sandals on her feet. With socks.

She clicked open the latch on the carrier and peeked inside. "Here, hon, let me help you." She took the carrier before I could answer and set the pugs free. "That's better."

They licked her hands, barking between slurps so hard, they bounced. Within a minute, they raced down the center aisle of the small shop. I've heard of kids in a candy store, but they had nothing on puppies in a pet store.

"I need supplies," I said. "I need to keep those two with me all the time. In the car, in meetings, at restaurants." I left out B&E's and stakeouts. "Do you have dog car seats?"

"We do," she said, and led me to a section along the back wall. "For those little guys, I'd go with this booster seat." She pulled out a nylon cube covered in soft orange padding.

With one eye on the dogs, I examined the latches and levers, listening while she explained the features.

"The seatbelt buckles through here, and you clip this to their harnesses like so," she said.

The puppies started barking in a crazy wild insane panic. I dropped the booster and raced to the end of the aisle. Colonel Mustard and Mrs. White crouched across from one another, a red rubber toy shoe between them. Kneeling down, butts in the air, yipping to warn of the inherent danger the three-inch shoe posed to all of society.

"I think I need the shoe," I said. "And beef sticks. And really big bells for their collars."

Fifteen minutes later, I knew more about dog safety than most vets. I bought a baby gate for their room (who knew such a thing existed?), four kinds of treats (they needed spoiling after their ordeal), and what might actually be a lifetime supply of Bullies. I also emerged with a fashionable leather carrier I could pass off as a purse (if I was an 1800s medicine woman).

Once secured in their new booster seat, raised so they could amply see out all windows and over doors, we cruised out of the lot and onto Cabana. Top down, wind rustling hair and ears, our collective nerves not nearly as jangled. I checked my rearview another eight dozen times, changing lanes often and randomly adjusting my speed to make sure we weren't being followed. I even stopped at the gas station. Topped off my tank and slowly washed my windshield. It gave me an opportunity to surreptitiously look through the glass for anyone lurking behind me. After taking a circuitous route to Oyster Cove, I backed into my driveway and dropped the baby gate and supplies in the garage, neatly arranging them near the door. Then we were off on our first adventure.

After a detour to McDonalds, we entered the Island Civic Complex which was located less than a mile from Oyster Cove Plantation and the tiniest airport still able to land planes. The county library occupied the west side and the Sea Pine Police Department took the east side. I parked the Mini in a fully legal standard spot beneath a towering oak and climbed out, juggling a cardboard to-go tray of drinks (one non-Pepsi cola beverage, one oj, one McCafe, and one Shamrock Shake) while wearing two pugs in a Baby Bjorn for dogs.

The volunteer at the desk took the proffered oj, but didn't buzz me in as usual. "I don't think Parker wants dogs in the bullpen, Elli."

"Who? These two angels?" I said. "They're fine."

They wiggled and squirmed, either trying to escape or crawl up my chest to kiss me.

"Are those the little guys who were pugnapped this morning?" she asked.

I clung to them, silently begging them to sit still. "Yes, and they're a little shaken up. I really do need to see Parker. I don't think she'll mind. It's her case. They're her case."

The volunteer opened the gate leading to the area behind the front counter, her arms outstretched in the universal sign for gimme. "I'll keep them penned here. It's a police station. They'll be fine. Promise."

I debated for all of the twenty-seven seconds it took to unstrap them from my body. "Thank you. I won't be long."

She buzzed me in without even glancing my way. She tossed two crumpled pieces of paper on the floor and it was puppies gone wild.

Once inside the inner sanctuary of the police department, I found my way to the bullpen. Cubes with standard desks and an assortment of office machinery took up most of the long blocky room. Larger offices, interrogation rooms, and holding cells lined the outer rim of the non-descript space.

Corporal Parker lifted her brow when she saw me and my array of morning beverages.

"For you," I said. "I wasn't sure which you preferred."

"Buttering me up for info won't work," she said.

She waited a beat, then took the Shamrock Shake, reaffirming my faith in humanity.

I grabbed the cola and sat in the side chair next to her desk. "Tell me everything you know."

Parker sipped her shake.

"Tell me everything Ransom said you could tell me."

"The car was stolen, no more info. But we're working on it.

The lieutenant ordered a full tech team to work on the car."

"That's a lot for a stolen car. He must think it's related to Lola."

"He thinks someone was waiting outside your cottage and kidnapped your dogs. He's concerned. You also went on a car chase this morning."

"That's fair," I said and leaned on her desk. "What about Lucy?"

"The crime scene at Lola's is clear," she said. "Looks like a surprise attack. The place was trashed. A bullet in the wall. Lucy may have pulled her gun. Might have been taken away from her. Perp shot her and ran. Her gun is missing, so be careful out there."

"Nice the lieutenant is sharing info, including me on the team," I said. "Any suspects? Witnesses? What else did you find on scene?"

"How is Lucy?" Parker asked, shutting the door on the lieutenant's help.

"She's in a coma. She's frail and small. Not the sassy PI who can conquer the world." I swigged from my coke too fast and the carbonation burned my throat. "I need to see Chef Carmichael."

"No can do. He's already at county and your name is on the Do Not Enter List."

"You do not have a Do Not Enter List."

Parker took a long sip of Shamrock Shake.

"When is the arraignment?" I asked.

"Set for Monday."

I nodded and stood and thanked her.

"You better get crackin'," she said as I walked away.

I loaded the pugs into their booster seat and dialed the county jail. Whilst I considered Corporal Parker an ally on the force, I found it prudent to spot check when needed. One minute later I clicked off. Turned out the jail did indeed have a Do Not Enter list and one Elliott Lisbon was at the tippy top for Thomas Carmichael. He really didn't want to talk to me. I took it as encouragement. If he were guilty, talking to me wouldn't make a difference. But he wanted to throw himself on his chef's knife, so to speak, and it was my job to stop him. It felt backward to work the case from this angle, but nothing had yet to be straightforward.

I sat in the driver's seat beneath a towering magnolia, pondering my day. It might include sneaking into a place or two. Sneaking required stealth. Colonel Mustard and Mrs. White did not know stealth. For two creatures barely larger than a pair of shoes, they made more noise than a pack of wild elephants stampeding across the plains of Africa.

I went to the Big House. I closed them in my office while I unloaded their supplies, then took them on a long walk around the back lawn. Once free of their leashes, they ran and ran, hopping and jumping on each other, rolling in the fresh cut grass. I sat on the steps that led from the pool to the lawn.

"Red."

Strong hands gripped my shoulders. He lifted me from sitting to standing and turned me to face him. He wrapped his arms around me tight, nearly clinging.

"You're okay?" he whispered in my ear.

"Yes, I'm shaken, but okay—"

He cut me off with a kiss. His lips warm. Demanding. A Marine on leave after six months in the desert. It intensified, then softened. He slowed and pulled back. Kissed my cheek, my forehead, my hair.

I looked up at him and touched his face.

"What the hell made you chase that car, Red? You could've been hurt."

I dropped my hand. "Don't lecture me. Was I supposed to let them steal Vivi's puppies? Hand them right over?"

"Well, Jesus, there's a multitude of choices between handing them right over and hunting down a criminal at ninety-two miles an hour."

"You weren't there. You don't know."

"I know you," he said. "You take too many risks. Too reckless."

"A risk worth taking. I'm not a child, Ransom. I can take care of myself. And these dogs. They are my responsibility."

"And you're mine."

"What does that mean? I'm not your responsibility."

He ran his hand through is hair. "Not what I meant to say."

"Then say what you mean."

"You scared the shit out of me."

"Scared the shit out of me, too." I watched the pugs on the grass. I still felt jittery, slightly off balance. "It's all so crazy. I don't know what to do."

"Don't chase cars." His words were playful, but his intense stare was not.

I held it. "Don't tell me what to do."

Colonel Mustard and Mrs. White sniffed their way along the high hedge, stopping by the water lily topiaries. They laid down near the Zen garden. The Colonel's head on Mrs. White's back.

"Do you still think Chef killed Lola?" I asked. "Because I do not see how he could've pugnapped two puppies from my bike basket this morning while still in jail. Or why he would've."

"Why would anyone?"

"For ransom, Ransom," I said. "To extort Vivi Ballantyne. Now you tell me why Chef would do that? You're the lieutenant who made the arrest. Practically on these grounds."

"By the way, the security team is here installing new

systems."

"Is that why you're here?"

"And to check on you. Make sure you're okay."

"I'm okay."

"I know the owner of the security company. It's his operation. He sent his top team. Cameras, motion detectors, the works. They'll set them up all over the Big House and the grounds."

"Not in the Zen garden," I said, watching the pugs rest near the last place Lola Carmichael took breath.

Ransom leaned back on his heels and put his hands in his pockets. "Not the Zen garden."

"I realize it might be safer here now, but it's also an invasion of privacy."

"I understand," he said. "You should know the team is going to your cottage next."

"What?" I said and stood board straight. "I didn't ask for that. And I do not want it. You cannot make those decisions for me."

"Not for you, with you."

"We did not discuss it."

"We are now," he said. "It's that or you're moving in with me."

"Those are the only choices?"

"For now. I have to sleep at night, too."

"In your own house," I said. "The one without an invasive security system installed without your consent."

He didn't budge. Not a face muscle, not an inch of his shoe. His jaw was clenched so tight, I thought his teeth might crack.

"Fine," I said. "But no cameras or motion detectors."

"Done."

I guess we aren't getting away to Fiji any time soon, I thought as he walked across the patio and into the Big House.

I joined the puppies near the Zen garden. They showed me their bellies, looking for scratches like a couple of cats. I obliged. It eased some tension. Some, not all. They rolled in the thick green grass, then popped up in tandem, barking and nipping. I clapped my hands and slow-jogged up the low steps toward the pool, their fuzzy paws close behind. We ran our way through the porch and into the kitchen.

"Surprise!" I said to Carla.

"I wondered if this visit included me." She wiped her hands on a towel, then bent to greet the puppies. "Am I on babysitting duty?"

"Pretty please? Is there somewhere you can watch them? Literally watch them all the time?"

"The solarium will work just fine," she said. "Never you mind."

The solarium was next to the kitchen. It overlooked the gardens, but more importantly, it had a huge picture window in the wall to also overlook the kitchen.

I hugged her tight, holding on an extra ten seconds. "Thank you, Carla. I'm grateful."

She shooed me out of her kitchen while I talked about toys and treats in my office. With the pugs safe (no one would dare take them from the Big House—not whilst the entire staff, security team, and Lieutenant Ransom were in residence), I was off.

For what felt like the nineteenth time in five days, I drove into Fisher's Landing Trailer Park and Yacht Club. I parked in the small lot near the entrance to the entertainment center and walked the wood ramp to Tug Boat Slim's.

Lunching residents and boaters filled the tables on the deck near the water. Likely the only place on Sea Pine Island where you were in full view of a sixty-foot sloop and a sixty-foot single wide.

Tug Jensen manned the teak bar inside, the fiberglass marlin perched high on the wall, though slightly askew. "Elli, what's going on?" he said, rushing around the long bar to greet me. "You okay? The dogs? Lucy?"

"I don't know what's going on, Tug," I said. "The world's gone crazy. Can we sit a minute?"

"Yeah, of course. Let's talk back here." I followed him to the corner near the rear door, the same table Lucy and I sat at the night before.

"Has it only been one night?" I asked. "I was just here with Lucy."

"How is she?"

I told him what the nurse told me. "You should go see her."

"Planning on it this afternoon," he said. "I heard someone tried to steal Lola's dogs?"

"Right out of my bike basket. Do you have any idea who would do that?"

"None. Who would snatch a couple of puppies? Or hurt Lucy. Or Lola." He rubbed his eyes. They were marred by dark marks in puffy half-moons beneath them.

"Were you and Lola close?"

He hollered to two staffers cleaning up tables from the party last night. Cases of hurricane glasses were stacked near the walkway to the kitchen. Finally, he turned to me. "Lola was so proud when Lucy got her private investigator's license. Kept a picture of it in her wallet. I think she attributed that to you for some reason."

"Lucy and I were friends once," I said. "When I first started helping Ballantyne donors with minor indiscretions a la Archy McNally style."

"Who?"

I shook my head. "A Lawrence Sanders character, not important."

"She mentioned Jupiter Jones," he said. "Figured he was on a case with you."

I laughed, a genuine laugh. "He's the lead investigator of the Three Investigators. As in Alfred Hitchcock. *The Mystery of the Stuttering Parrot.*"

"Ah," he said with a short laugh. "That girl was something."

"Which one? Lola or Lucy?"

"Both."

I let a minute click by before asking again. "You and Lola were friends? I know she was your landlord. Seems like you two might be close. She lives within shouting distance of your deck."

"I don't like to get too personal, but I know you're picking up where Lucy left off. Someone has to find what happened to our Lola. Just wish it wasn't so."

"Me too."

He stared at his hands on the table. "Lola and me dated now and again. Off and on. Right now, to make it worse, we were off. Sometimes things got complicated with the trailer park."

"With her being the landlord?"

"With her being behind on the mortgage."

"So you knew about that?"

"It's a trailer park on an island. You can't fish this pond without every sardine, oyster, and guppy knowing your business."

"I can't even follow that."

"We'd all seen the notices. I told her I'd lend her the money. Even if I had to take out a loan. She wouldn't even hear it."

"She was too proud?" I asked.

He paused before answering. He asked a server for a couple of waters before turning back to me. "Spring, flat, sparkling, tap? Or tea?"

"Spring would be great."

He hollered for two spring waters. "You were saying?"

"I asked if Lola was too proud to take money from you."

"Definitely proud. And a perceptive business woman."

"Oh?"

"I wanted to buy the land the bar sits on. I've been leasing it for years. Buying it was win-win. She'd get enough cash to pay down her mortgage and I'd finally have security. With all the development going on, I didn't like leasing. A new owner could sell the place out from under me."

"But Lola didn't go for it," I said.

"Elli, the woman lost her shit," he said. "Thought I didn't trust her. Accused me of all kinds of things including colluding with her bank."

"Charter bank?" I asked. "I don't understand."

"It's complicated. I don't actually have the money to buy the land, so I'd need to get a loan. We both bank at Charter. No surprise since most of the island banks there. Even if I offered her a million dollars, she would've said no. She didn't want to hear it."

"When was this?"

"Big fight on Saturday morning. Right before I handed you the marlin. And before you ask, I didn't see her at the party. Well, just a minute, but she wasn't talking to me."

"Where did you see her?"

"Talking to Chef. And no, I don't think he did it."

"Was he by the Zen garden? It's near the pool."

"No, by his booth."

A server dropped two glasses of water on the table with a pair of straws and left us alone.

I took a long sip and sat back. "How well do you know Jessie Carmichael?"

"Well enough. We weren't friends. Their divorce was a while ago. He hurt Lola, but she could take care of herself." He drank from the cup as if it was filled with bourbon, or at least wished it was. "Used to, anyway."

"You think he could've done this?" I said.

"I don't like the guy, but I don't see why he'd do it."

"Money. Isn't that what it's always about?"

"He doesn't seem that ambitious. Too much work for a guy like that."

"And you? I'm sorry to ask, but—"

He called to the two servers cleaning the tables in our section. "You see me at the party on Saturday over at the cook-off?"

"Of course," one said.

"I ever leave our booth, once I got there?"

One of the staffers looked at me, then back at Tug. "No. This about Lola?"

"I know it's hard," I said. "Just crossing all the t's."

"He never left the booth. I never saw Lola either. Wish I had."

After they walked away, Tug leaned on the table. "What's going to happen to Lucy?"

"Nurse said she's going to be okay. Might take a week or so."

"I mean now that Lola's gone. That changes things."

"Indeed it does."

I stood and thanked him. He stopped me on my way out. "I'm interim park manager. With Lola gone. You let me know if you see anything out there." With a head nod toward the trailer park, he turned to the bar, away from me.

With my messenger bag slung crossbody, I slowly left Tug's and walked over to Lola's. I took a peek inside her trailer with the hide-a-key I never re-hid. A strip of crime scene tape was still stuck to the door. It flapped in the early morning light breeze.

It was quiet inside the trailer. Still. Abandoned. Smudges of fingerprint powder marred various surfaces, leaving the once-cheery home looking sad and old. Tired and empty. The bullet hole in the wall was marked with tape and a slip of paper. I peered throughout, careful not to touch or step or knock into anything.

Two minutes later, I locked the door behind me and walked to the yellow rental next door.

Since one of the keys on Lucy's ring worked, I was happy to not have to break and enter another trailer home. Literally. I mean, I had the key, just not the permission.

The single wide was clean and uncluttered. It was a mishmosh of seventies and eighties décor without a single personal touch to make it homey or welcoming. Just a short-term rental no larger than a mouse hole.

The kitchen appliances were faded pink. The stove with four tiny burners, the fridge no taller than chin-height. With the exception of the flooring (speckled rubber-tile in the kitchen/living room, matted shaggy carpet in the bedroom), every surface was coated in wood. Or a wood-ish product. Even the ceiling.

I searched the drawers and cupboards, of which there were plenty. They just weren't large. Random-aged appliances (Mr. Coffee without the glass carafe, waffle iron coated in grime, electric can opener with a jacked-up cord), plus murky bottles, old books, milk glass lampshades. Everything looked sticky (and likely stuck to the decades-old contact paper).

No phone or laptop. I didn't know if Lucy had even brought a laptop with her from Dallas, but she had a phone. She'd given me the number. A charger was plugged in next to the bed. The thin cord draped carelessly across the mattress edge as if flung there after use. I dug her card out of my bag and dialed the number. It rang in my ear, but not in the trailer.

A quick search of the bedroom section netted me a single tidbit: A framed picture of Lola and Lucy on the nightstand, probably something Lucy brought with her or something she took from Lola's.

Nothing else. I could not believe Lucy did not have a notebook or a copy of Lola's will or a scrap of anything. Lucy was a legitimate PI and working her mother's case was her singular focus. Something had to be here.

Unless the shooter took it, along with her phone.

I started over.

Back to the front. I unzipped the velveteen chair cushion, lifted the vinyl dinette seats, tapped the rusted chrome, raised the shag carpet, crawled on the rubber kitchen floor looking for flipped corners or mismatched tiles, swashed myself repeatedly with my hand-sani bottle until it was nearly empty.

Still nothing. I sat on Lucy's bed, fiddling with her phone charger. Her trailer didn't look tossed. It looked neat. Nothing dumped or ripped or jammed into place.

"Dear, clever, Lucy," I said to the empty room. "Where oh where did you hide your goods? What one thing is not like the other?"

Snap! I went back to the kitchen to the cupboard in the corner between the stove and the sink. The books, both Alfred Hitchcock and the Three Investigators, like we used to read. Like the identical ones in her mother's trailer. *The Mystery of the Stuttering Parrot. The Mystery of the Whispering Mummy.* I'm a super fan, but even I didn't keep a duplicate set. It meant something. Especially after Lucy's earlier Jupiter Jones reference.

I climbed up on the counter, teetering on the Formica, and moved the books from the shelf. The bottom did indeed stick to the contact paper. When I pushed the paper down, the surface was slightly uneven. After a gentle pull, it lifted from the cabinet bottom. Before I stuck my hand into the dark, tacky gap, I used my flashlight app to brighten the space. A thin hardcover book, almost like a yearbook, sat flat beneath the exposed paper. The word "record" was stamped on front. With all three books in hand, I hopped down and sat at the dinette.

The record book was the rental ledger for Fisher's Landing. The earliest entries were from two years ago. I'm not an accountant, but it looked fairly organized. Each line written in pencil, a trailer lot number with the amount paid and date. One thing stood out right away: Imogene Metwally paid rent on four trailers, three in the back row. The rental row where Lola kept her flop trailers. Starting eight months before Lola died.

I thumbed through the rest of the ledger and Lola's will fell out. A brief three pages, folded in half, stapled in the corner, signed the day she died. A quick read told me nothing surprising, but I'd reread later just to be sure. I tucked it back inside the ledger.

Deciding thumbing worked, I picked up the *Whispering Mummy* and flipped through the pages. The final third of the pages didn't flip. They didn't move. With light prodding, two pages unstuck, uncovering a hidey hole. Lucy had glued together the last pages of the book and cut out a rectangle, then wedged in a compact diary.

Every entry started *Dear Mom*. The ink on the last entry's words were blurred, as if from spilled tears. I quickly shut the journal. I wrapped the attached elastic band around it twice. Much too personal for any eyes but Lucy's.

The *Stuttering Parrot* netted similar results. Only this time, a small notebook sat inside. Random words, initials, odd spacing, fairytale character names. Even though I didn't immediately understand its meaning, I knew it meant something. And I could figure it out.

I tucked everything into my messenger bag: the ledger, the

will, the hollowed out books, and the framed picture. With a last look around, including a peek out the windows to check for wandering neighbors and fluttering curtains. I slipped outside and into the Mini.

The sound of colorful shiny flags snapping in the wind from across the street taunted me. Reminding me of unfinished confrontations.

Only took forty-five seconds to scoot me and the Mini from one parking lot to the other. I stomped up the steps of the sales trailer and flung open the door.

"Chas Obermeyer," I said. "You are a liar."

I was hoping for a room full of potential clients who would gasp at my dramatic accusation, but only Chas and Bitsy were inside. Neither gasped. But at least Chas was there and not at the bank.

"What do you want, Elliott?" Chas asked.

"Lola's mortgage was not paid anonymously," I said. "You straight up lied to my face."

"I'm protecting my client," Chas said.

"I have written permission."

"I'm not losing my job by giving out confidential client information. Not off a piece of scratch paper anyone could've written. I told you it wasn't legal."

"Then why not say that?"

"Because you're a damn dog with a bone. You'd twist my arm or ask for favors. Screw that. I got enough on my plate and I'm not doing a single favor to help that witch Jane Hatting."

"This is for Vivi."

"Well, now, let's all calm down," Bitsy said. She stepped next to Chas to form a united front. "Perhaps we can talk to Edward and Vivi over dinner. Shall we set a date?"

"They are in Greenland," I said.

"Not forever," Bitsy said. "You know, the Oglevie dinner

party is this week. I'm sure they'd love to have the Ballantyne's over. I'll just make a note to call Cherie—"

"They don't want a dinner party, Bitsy," I said. "They want me to find out what happened to Lola."

"It can't hurt, Elliott," Bitsy said. "I'm only trying to help."

"Wonderful," I said. "Where were you both on Saturday? At the Big House?"

"Wait, you can't think—" Bitsy said.

"Don't say anything," Chas said. "Talk to my lawyer."

"Now you need a lawyer?" I turned to Bitsy. "What will Vivi think?"

"Neither of us were even at the Irish Spring," she said. "I hated to miss it. I knew Vivi and Edward were out of town, so I didn't think they'd mind. But we were getting ready to open the sale trailer. It was a Saturday. The most popular home shopping day of the week."

"We're done helping," Chas said. "We're not getting involved. Not me, not my wife, not my bank."

"But you know exactly who paid off Lola's mortgage?" I asked.

Death glare.

"And you're not going to tell me?"

"Do you want him to throw away his entire career?" Bitsy said. "He's worked hard for his position at the bank. This sliver of information can't be that important." She looked torn between standing by her man and her man standing in the way of her social status.

"Solving this murder is important," I said.

"To you, not me," Chas said.

"Chas, this is imperative."

"Everything with you is imperative," Chas said. "Life or death. It's getting ridiculous."

"Lola Carmichael is dead and her daughter was shot last

night and is now in a coma. Someone did that in Lola's trailer home," I said with a dramatic arm swing toward Fisher's Landing. "Right there."

Bitsy paled, but Chas didn't flinch. "I'm not budging. It's my bank. If you want the information, you'll need a warrant."

I looked from Chas, with his hands fisted on his hips, to Bitsy, with her hands clutching her pearls, then marched out in disdain so they'd know exactly what I thought of them.

A warrant? No one was giving me a warrant. PIs-in-training were not issued warrants. Police lieutenants were. But police lieutenants didn't share info with PIs-in-training, especially lieutenants who took confessions from chefs at face value.

I sat in my car stewing. With the top down, I had a clear view of Fisher's Landing. I could see Tug Boat Slim's. A couple of golf carts parked at the entertainment center. I couldn't see Lola's trailer or the Winnebago.

I took in an enormous breath and blew out a gigantic, lip fluttering sigh. Did it actually matter who paid off Lola's mortgage? I didn't know. But what I did know: It's a PI-in-training's job to collect as much information as possible, then decide what mattered. I stared through the windshield.

I had a ledger and a coded notebook filled with intel, but I still needed more info. And I couldn't just sit there all day.

THIRTEEN

(Day #5: Wednesday Afternoon)

With a big floppy hat on my head, I zoomed down Cabana Boulevard to Marsh Grass Road and took the turn on two wheels. Figuratively. The afternoon sunshine warmed my nose as I kept my eyes on the road, occasionally glancing to the right, looking for my destination.

I soon passed the Gullah Catfish Café and the entrance to Mamacita's herb garden. I spent several afternoons last year in her maze of leafy greens and poisonous plants. Some memories pleasant, others not so much.

It wasn't a mile later that I saw an old painted sign close to the road's edge with Ida Claire written in faded green paint. The barely legible words "Southern Kitchen" were scrawled near the bottom. I eased into the gravel lot, parking near the door. Vintage diner signs decorated the picture windows sporting phrases like "Best Coffee in Town" and "Good Eats Here." A trio of big-bellied cats greeted me when I approached the screen door. Two looked at me with droll disinterest, one howled and pawed at me as if my pockets were crammed with tuna.

She may have been warning me. A half dozen ceiling fans whirred in random locations, moving muggy air from one section to another. No hum from a central air system or rattle from a wall unit sounded. While it was only in the low eighties outside, that was still warm enough to feel stifling inside.

A woman with thick blue eye shadow and a ring in her nose showed me to a table on the far side of the long room. The tabletop had torn pages from classic Southern novels decoupaged beneath a thick layer of plastic. Pencil illustrations and magazine covers kept them company. A long counter with vinyl-topped stools ran the length of the diner near the kitchen. Rusted toys and metal signs decorated a shelf close to the ceiling.

"Miss Elliott," Imogene said as she plopped down a glass of ice water and a straw. "You're here."

"I am indeed," I said with a friendly smile. One that said I'm delighted to be here even though it's one thousand degrees and ceiling fans are dispersing dust particles willy nilly from table to dish at a languid pace and I'd forgotten to wear my hazmat suit. "What's good for lunch? I'm kind of starving."

Imogene wiped her hands on her apron of her uniform, the kind Alice wore when working at Mel's Diner, and pointed to one item on a grease-spotted menu. "You have to try the chicken and waffles. Our best seller by far. Everyone comes here for 'em. Matter of fact, we could probably just be Ida Claire's Chicken and Waffle House and sell nothing else and we'd all be rich."

"With that kind of recommendation, I'll take an order. And a Pepsi. Large. Enormous. Super size me."

"You got it," she said and picked up the flimsy menu.

The diner was quiet. Afternoon mid-week, probably not their busiest hour. Two women sat near the door gabbing over slices of pie and a glass pitcher of lemonade. Three people sat at the counter, the requisite two-stool distance between them.

"You have a minute?" I asked Imogene when she brought me a towering red plastic cup filled with cola and crushed ice. "I need to ask about Lola, and I don't mean to upset you at work, but it could be important."

"Of course," she said, without even looking at her co-workers or boss for permission. "We're slow. Besides, I've been crying for days. Folks 'round here probably happy to have me out of their hair for a spell."

"I'm assisting Lucy with Lola's estate and I noticed you pay rent on several different trailers at Fisher's Landing."

"I do. Or did. Well, still do, not sure what I'll do now." She reached into her apron pocket and pulled out a men's handkerchief, circa whatever year it was when men carried cotton handkerchiefs, and blotted her neck and cleavage. "One trailer's mine, of course. For living. Had it since I moved in there. I own the trailer and rent the spot. The other three's on flop row. I rent the trailers and the spots, so's the payments are double, though still not as much as I pay for the one I'm living in. Those flop trailers aren't snazzy."

"What do you do with them?"

"Rent them to locals. I clean them, turn them, and collect the rent. My son handles most of it, really, including repairs, of which there are plenty. I don't think any one of them trailers is younger than me. And I'm no spring chicken."

"Is there that much business for rental trailers? Especially in a place called flop row? Doesn't sound very profitable. Or safe."

She fanned herself with the hankie. "It's definitely not the most profitable, but safe. Austin knows a bunch of surfers. They like the short-term rentals and we like the cash. They'll be here through the summer, then move on down to Florida for the rest of the season. We'll see 'em again in the fall."

"Why didn't Lola rent them herself?"

"That flop row was really going downhill." Imogene lowered her voice. "Not to speak ill of Lola. It wasn't her fault or anything. I don't mean to imply such a thing. She was doing the best she could do. Those trailers were just sitting empty going on two years almost. I took them off her hands. It was win-win. She got rent and I got cash."

Imogene must have seen my eyes twinkle at her mention of extra cash. Money always topped every investigator's list of motives.

"They're still flop trailers and I'm still slinging hash," she added. "Not that much money rolling in. It's spending cash for Austin mostly. Besides, Lola didn't know what to do with those flops. Didn't have the money to invest in nicer trailers." She sighed from down deep. "That park was everything to her. She had plans, you know. Spruce it up, expand the entertainment center. Put in some newer models to rent. They make them to look like real houses now."

The bell above the diner door jingled and we both swiveled to look. Imogene dabbed her upper lip with her hankie and smiled at her son, Austin, as he walked straight to our table.

"Brought the car by, Ma," he said. "How late's your shift? I got time to eat?"

"Austin, mind your manners," she said with a nudge. "Say hello to Miss Elliott. You met the other morning."

"Oh sure, hello," he said.

A counter bell rang from the kitchen and Imogene snapped her fingers. "Your lunch."

Austin stood by the table, his hands in his pockets, slowly rocking back and forth.

"Please join me." I gestured to an empty chair across from me.

He sat in the one next to mine and hollered at Imogene as she approached. "Hey Ma, can I get a coke? And lunch?"

Imogene set a platter in front of me and I nearly moaned right out loud. I was expecting a thick wide waffle stacked with fried chicken smothered in goopy gravy. What she placed before me would truly make our Chef Carla jealous. Crisp chicken bites sat atop petite waffles. A drizzle of creamy syrup sauce delicately swiveled onto each pairing. A sophisticated balance of sweet and savory, crunchy and crisp, in every bite. I was a third of the way through the meal before I remembered I wasn't dining alone.

"So Austin, your mom tells me you're a handyman," I said between bites.

"Handyman?"

"For the rental trailers," Imogene said. She set a plate of chicken and waffles in front of Austin, along with two big icy drinks. She joined us and sipped. "I was telling her about our rentals in flop row."

"Oh that," he said. "It's just part-time for me, and only cause my mom needs the help. I manage a golf course."

"Really? Which one?"

"Captain Blackbeard's over on Cabana."

I nodded politely, grateful my mouth was full. I didn't know people referred to miniature golf as a golf course.

"There's a big tournament tomorrow out at Vista Lakes. It'd be great if you could come out."

Now Vista Lakes had a real course. A real private course. The area around Sea Pine Island had more golf holes per capita than anywhere in the United States. You could golf a different course every single day for two months and never repeat. Or something like that. I didn't golf.

"I'll actually be there already," I said. "Not playing, though. The Ballantyne is one of the sponsors. You golf there, too?"

"I'm a caddy. Saving up for my own course. I'm still working on investors, but it's going to be stellar." He pointed his fork at me. "The Ballantyne Foundation would be prime to sponsor a hole at the place. Or maybe even invest. Hey, we could call it the Ballantyne Club. Wouldn't that be something? The plans I'm working on would impress you, for sure."

I took a large bite of waffled chicken and made positive-sounding noises. I didn't think Austin understood how charities worked. Or at least how the Ballantyne Foundation worked. We were only one of the many sponsors at the tournament at Vista Lakes. Sponsoring a tournament was one thing. Owning a course was a different league.

Imogene cleared our plates after we'd nearly licked them clean. "Getcha anything else, Miss Elliott?"

"I couldn't eat another thing."

"I'll take a slice of apple," Austin said. "With cheddar on top."

"Your mom tells me you know Lucy," I said.

"Yeah, when we were little," Austin said. "We hung out some. But then, you know, high school."

"I knew her back then, too, though not when she was little," I said. "She's a good one."

"Yeah. I've been meaning to talk to her. Been waiting for the right moment. I know she's got a lot going on with her mom and all. I'm going to invite her to the tournament tomorrow. Show her my plans for the new course."

"Lucy's in the hospital," I said.

"What? The hospital?" Imogene said, setting a slice of pie in front of Austin.

"She was shot last night."

They both looked at me as if I'd started speaking Spanish and they couldn't understand a word I was saying.

"Shot?"

"With a gun?"

"She's in a coma, but the doctor says she'll be okay," I said. "Did either of you see her last night after the wake?"

"No," Imogene said, her voice barely above a whisper. "I didn't even get the chance to give my proper condolences. We seen her at Tug's and was making our way over, but then she just up and left."

"Yeah, I thought I'd see her later," Austin said. "Man, I never shoulda waited so long."

"You need to visit her," Imogene said to Austin. "We'll go today."

"I don't think she'd even remember me, Ma."

She patted his slumpy shoulder. "She'll remember you just fine. I need to clean up my station, then we'll go." Imogene turned to me. "Lunch is on the house. I'm so sorry to keep meeting you like this." She took her apron off and walked toward the kitchen.

I didn't think the hospital would let Imogene and Austin into Lucy's room, but I didn't want to discourage it. I left a tip on the table and said my thank yous and goodbyes, then climbed into the Mini.

A trip to visit Lucy was on my own agenda, but I'd wait until the end of the day. Let other people visit with her first. They could afford to spend the day bedside. I could not. I needed to spend the day finding out who was out to hurt the Carmichaels. Lola was dead, Lucy was shot, and Chef was in jail.

It briefly occurred to me that the same individual may not have committed these crimes. But that thought flitted out of my brain as quickly as it flitted in. No family suffered that much vehemence, with back-to-back violent outbursts in four days, without it being perpetrated by the same person. At least not on Sea Pine Island.

FOURTEEN

(Day #5: Wednesday Afternoon)

I returned to the Island Civic Complex, but parked on the library side this time. Massive oaks and crape myrtles covered the lot. I put the top up, not wanting my seats to be covered in tree debris when I returned.

Deidre Burch manned the information desk at the far wall of the cramped room. She placed colorful bookmarks in worn hardcovers as I approached.

"Elli Lisbon, what brings you by?" she asked, peering over her orange readers.

"The computer, any computer," I said, then nodded to the one in the corner. "By any, I mean that one."

"You ever find anything out about Chef Carmichael's corned beef?" At my surprised yet discreet look, she added, "I figured that's what you wanted at lunch after Zibby told me Julia told you about Lola's recipe in Chef's cookbook. When you were asking if I tasted both pots of gold at the cook-off."

"Man this island is small. Tiny. Miniscule. Like living on a commune."

"One big happy family." Deidre jotted my name on the computer signup sheet with a flourish. "All yours. You let me know if you crack the case while you're here."

"Will do." I walked away happy she hadn't asked me why I was using the old CPU in the public library rather than my not as old laptop in my private home. It seemed too exhausting to explain my apprehensions. First with would-be pugnappers lurking in the shrubs outside my cottage. Second with a security team wiring the walls and windows inside my cottage. Though with Deidre's connection inside the island gossip network, she probably didn't ask because she probably already knew.

Waiting for the aging desktop to boot up, I set out supplies on the square desk: my favorite blue pen, my notebook, and Lucy's notebook. I took my time paging through her notes.

The arbitrary words and phrases still looked random, but I slowly began to see order. It seemed as if Lucy would jot things as they came to her. A stream of consciousness note-taking strategy. Capitalization and punctuation did not get in her way. Casual references to trigger her own memory, but designed to confuse the crap out of a nosy Nellie who might end up sneaking a peek at her notes. All written in barely legible, scratchy handwriting.

Based on the number of pages, I guessed it was her suspect book. (I did not have a suspect book, just a normal notebook. I made a mental note to perhaps create a suspect book.) From what I could deduce, Lucy created codenames for suspects in her cases. Some got a full page, other's a half. Codename at the top, several short lines below. Each with a set of asterisks. Either doodles, dividing lines, ranking system, or times she interviewed them? Each set of names were themed: Mickey, Minnie, Donald, Daisy, and Goofy. Scarlett, Rhett, Melanie, Ashley, and Bonnie. Perhaps each separate case got a theme.

The last few pages were dedicated to fairytales: Little Red Riding Hood, Geppetto, Jiminy Cricket, and Rumpelstiltskin. The theme for her mother's case? Each followed the same pattern:

Rumplstiskn
* * * * *

mt: money
Money, money money
team or solo? Track Wed.

Jimny Crickt
* * *

mt: apprval?
cold shoulder, access denied
end scene.

Queen of Hrts
* * * * *

mt: ladder/ruinatn
w/ geppetto t (again m)
trade up or trade secrets?

Red Riding Hd
* * * *

mt: money
visit the wolf m
empty bundles??
deleted browser histry?

Hook
* * *

mt: money
rocket man! (fly that kite)
3h genius man
Karma!!!
Need f/up W

Geppetto
* * * * *
mt: money
strong overture
w/ queen

Granny
* * *
mt: love
too close

These weren't random fairytale characters. They all lived in Storybrooke of *Once Upon a Time* fame, a tv show I introduced to Ransom. (He never missed an episode but would never admit that outside my cottage walls.)

Which meant, taking Lucy's gibberishy list literally, she had seven suspects. But I did not have seven suspects. I didn't have any. At least not any I'd taken time to write down and seriously consider. It'd only been four days.

Chef had to be one of Lucy's suspects. But which one? I needed to decipher each codename and figure out what all those stars meant. Lucy must have felt she needed an extra code. I wondered why. I also wondered how secure my own notebook was. I'd never once considered coding my jots and ruminations, nor thought anyone would steal it. The difference between PI-ing in Dallas vs. PI-in-training in Sea Pine, or difference in experience?

I carefully copied the info from Lucy's book to mine. Each line, each letter, exactly as she wrote them. As I may have a very mild form of OCD, I didn't worry about missing a dotted i or crossed t or weirdly spelled half-word.

It took an hour to recreate her notebook, at least the *Once*

Upon a Time pages. That way I could jot my own notes without disturbing hers. Like a diary, a PI's notebook was too personal to add outside commentary. Lucy had full suspect pages after only three days. How did she get so much so fast? How did she figure it all out and then not write that part down?

I booted up the Google box and felt a burst of confidence for the first time in days. I realized that Lucy likely did write that part down, the part where she figured out the killer. I just had to crack her code.

I loved the internet. I'm not saying I believe everything on there or it's my sole news source, but type in anything and you'll get seven million responses.

Which made cracking Lucy's code not as difficult as she may have thought it was.

I found not one, but two different Wiki-type websites with full descriptions of each *Once Upon A Time* character. As a fan of the show, I had a basic grasp, but basic wouldn't crack diddlysquat.

Rumple: He's all about the money. Mr. Gold, the man who barters, trades, and minds the pawn shop, a desperate man's bank.

Bank! I wrote a name in my notebook next to Lucy's Rumple code: Chas.

Jiminy: The son of con artists who wants the honest life, yet still tries to please the family.

Easy enough. Chef confessed to protect his brother. All about the family. If Chas is all about the money, Chef is all about the family.

Queen of Hearts: She married for money/stature and wanted her daughter to do the same (even killed to make it happen).

This was a harder one. Jane came to mind. Though she was unmarried and had built-in social status. Plus, getting real, she's the Evil Queen if ever there was one. I made a short list of women I'd encountered so far: Lucy, Imogene, Bitsy. With my own asterisk next to Bitsy, I marked her as the most likely Queen of Hearts because her pink car was in Tug's lot the morning of the Irish Spring.

Little Red Riding Hood: On the show, she was nice outside, but a terrorizing wolf inside. Worked as a waitress at the local diner.

Imogene? She's a waitress. Seemed nice outside, much more questionable inside? I put her name next to Red Riding Hood's.

Hook: A swashbuckler with inner demons, trying for redemption.

Obvious choice is Austin, Imogene's son, since he worked at Captain Blackbeard's Mini Golf. But Lucy hadn't even seen him yet, at least according to Imogene and Austin. Was he enough of a suspect to make the list? Was Lucy's suspect list accurate or filled with red herrings? I jotted his name next to Hook, but left extra space to update.

Geppetto: He's a woodworker, carpenter, and handyman. He wanted a son, so he carved one from wood.

No idea. I made a short list of men I'd encountered and not yet assigned: Tug, Jessie. Lucy said her mission was to prove her father killed her mother. That meant Jessie was someone on this list.

Granny: She owned the diner in Storybrooke and her family fell victim to the wolf.

Is Granny a literal granny or true to the *Once* character? Would Lucy suspect her own grandmother? Perhaps a sly reference to Tug? He owned the restaurant where everyone at Fisher's Landing, including Lola, hung out. I wrote both Virginia and Tug next to this one.

That gave me three solid identifications: Chas/Rumple,

Chef/Jiminy, Imogene/Red Riding; two maybes: Austin/Hook, Tug/Virginia/Granny. That left two unassigned: Queen of Hearts and Geppetto.

I left plenty of room for my entire analysis of Lucy's suspect book to be completely off, but I needed to start somewhere. Though the method of assigning character codes and secret stars seemed oddball, it also gave an alternative perspective. One could detach completely while staying engaged. It created an urgent puzzle out of ordinary practices. Not only did Lucy impress me, she was also teaching me. I didn't want to let her down.

My entire life revolved around feeding a pair of pugs. I wanted to continue decrypting Lucy's notebook, but it had to wait. I also wanted to stop by Island Memorial, but that also had to wait. The Colonel Mustard and Mrs. White demanded to be fed at regular intervals since they could not handle the task themselves. They assaulted me with nips at my ankles when I greeted them in the solarium. I scooped them up, one in each hand, and in gratitude, they assailed me with barks and yips.

Carla assured me they'd remained secure from ne'er-do-wells. They also quite enjoyed being close to so much food. She noted she may or may not have snuck them treats all afternoon.

Once home, I kept them bundled in the baby sling strapped tight to my chest while I carefully checked each room. I carried a baseball bat. Stacks of alarm system booklets were neatly arranged on the countertop.

I wasn't actually too worried about a nefarious prowler waiting to pounce on me or my puppies. Mainly because this joker was an amateur. Or they had hired an amateur. Someone like Virginia Carmichael. A shortcut move to hire an idiot relative. A cousin, an in-law, a stepchild twice removed who showed up at family gatherings where no one remembered how they were related. There'd been no plan, no solid escape route. I nearly caught them in a Mini Coop in broad daylight with a pair of police cruisers only minutes behind.

Also abating my fears: one of those police cruisers was parked at the foot of my driveway. Unmanned, but still intimidating.

After declaring the cottage safe, dinner commenced: cereal for the human, crunchies for the pugs. I was nearly to the bottom of my box of Honey Nut Cheerios. I'd soon need to swing by the grocery, I thought as I shook the box, then peered inside at the random o's and honey nut dust, wondering if I could make it another day. I hated shopping almost as much as I hated cooking.

After a long walk (the pugs would've trotted the circumference of the island three times over if I let them), we returned to the cottage. It was early evening. The sun no longer bright, the moon a faint white stencil against a darkening blue sky. I secured the miniature eating machines behind their new baby gate after mandatory belly rubbing, ball tossing, and rope tugging.

I needed to call Ransom. We had yet to speak since our disagreement over my cottage's security plan and I hated to be the one to call first. Especially to ask for a favor. I knew I was being stubborn, but I also knew I needed a favor.

I dialed and he answered on the fourth ring. "Ransom."

"Red."

"Can you babysit?" I asked.

"I know how, if that's what you're asking."

"That's not what I'm asking. I want to visit Lucy, but I don't want to leave the pugs alone."

"Did you see the new security pad? It's by the door."

I wandered to the front door where a shiny new alarm pad

was mounted on the wall. A sheet of paper was taped next to it with a bullet list of instructions written in large letters. "I see it."

"Set the alarm before you leave. And again when you get home. There are two different codes. One for leaving, one for home. I'm texting them now."

I glanced at the code when it beeped on my phone. "I see that, too. But I still need a babysitter."

"Peek out the front door at the police car."

"I'm not leaving them here alone."

I could've heard his exhale from two hundred feet away. "I can't help you tonight. I'm on a case."

"Where are you?"

"I can't say."

"Chef is in jail. If this case is closed, then what are you doing?"

"Calm down. Chef Carmichael is not the only criminal on this island."

I cringed at him calling Chef a criminal and at my overreaction. I knew I was crowding his space, stepping over the line. But I was finding it hard to balance. He knew things that could help me, but he couldn't help me, and I knew I needed to just let it be.

"Fine," I said. "I get it."

"I'll call you later."

I knew I could figure it out without him. Because he was certainly trying to figure it out without me. I went upstairs to my roommates. "Plan B."

I gathered them up, squirming, licky, excited, and loaded them into the passenger seat of the Mini. Without a hat atop my head, my hair whipped in the briny air, leaving my mop half curly, half wavy, but fully carefree. It felt good. It felt as if I were getting somewhere. I leaned over to my traveling companions tucked safely in their booster. "We're getting somewhere."

I phoned Sid along the way. "I need help with a smuggling operation," I said when she answered.

"Drugs or money?"

"Dogs."

"Go on."

"I want to visit Lucy, and I think it will do her good to see Colonel Mustard and Mrs. White. To smell their puppy breath."

"She's in a coma."

"She can still smell."

"Meet me in the lobby," Sid said. "Wait. Make it the lot out front, but in a spot off to the side."

"Be there in ten."

I parked at Island Memorial beneath an oversized magnolia tree. Its thick waxy leaves barely fluttered in the light breeze. I unbuckled our belts as Sid rolled a cart out of the automatic entrance doors.

"Load them up," she said when she reached us. "I've got a cloth here."

The booster fit on the second tier of the metal cart, the pink linen cloth barely covering them. The bottom of the nylon booster showed, but I doubted anyone would recognize it as such. They commenced barking in the pink darkness.

"Well, that won't do," Sid said.

"I came prepared." I gently placed a long Bully in the booster and the barking ceased. "Like a bottle to a baby."

We rolled the cart into the lobby and down the long hall, chatting overly loud to cover any gnawing sounds.

"You ready for the brunch Friday?" I asked.

"As I'll ever be," she said. "I think this is my last year as the board president. With the hospital, the hospice thrift shop, my real estate career, and Milo, I may have to lop off some commitments. The Suffrage Society being at the top of the list."

"I hear you, sister." I punched the up button and we waited

for the elevator car.

"It doesn't help that Jane is this year's recipient of Woman of the Year," Sid said. "Or that she'd like to join the board next year."

"Reason enough," I said. "Who needs that kind of noise?"

The elevator door slid open. We tried to enter, but the front cart wheels got caught on the gap between the hospital floor and the elevator floor. It bumped forward toward Sid, then lurched backward toward me.

Barking ensued. Muffled frantic yips shook the cart.

"What are you doing?" Sid asked.

"I'm pulling," I said.

"Well, I'm lifting," she said.

"What's wrong with this elevator that the floors don't line up? This can't be safe."

"Just push and worry about safety later."

"Sure, sure. Like when we're inside?"

I pushed too hard and the cart smacked into the side of the elevator. The doors binged as they closed in, then again when they shimmied back into their slots.

A surgeon in a stripped scrub cap walked by. She side-eyed the cart, but didn't slow. "Sid," she said with a head tip.

"Dr. Crenshaw," Sid said.

We coordinated our lift and push and settled into the empty elevator car, soothing the pugs until they stopped yipping. Once it was quiet, we eased up to the third floor.

Dinnertime had long since passed, most visitors had gone for the night. We nodded to the guard outside Lucy's door, then eased the cart into her room. The same nurse from the night before stuck her head in. "What's in the cart?"

I looked at Sid. I hadn't thought that far ahead. If someone were to flat out ask.

"Puppies," Sid said. She raised the pink cloth like a curtain.

"Have you ever?"

The nurse leaned down and lifted the booster from the shelf. The puppies licked her hands clean and still wanted more.

"It's okay they're here?" I asked.

"No, but I won't tell if you won't," she said. "We've had dog days before in the children's wing. Nothing like puppy love to brighten spirits. But if they start barking, you'll be run out of here right quick."

The nurse left and Sid helped me hold the pugs at Lucy's bedside. They licked her hands and sniffed her arms. Mrs. White whimpered.

"I think she knows Lucy," I said.

"Did Lucy ever meet the pugs?"

"She delivered them to me, but she could've only spent an hour or two with them. Maybe Lucy smells like her mother."

We tucked the pugs back into the booster with their half-chewed Bully and set it on the floor.

Sid hugged me quick. "Let me know if you need me."

"I always need you," I said. She started to leave, but I stopped her. "I let Lucy fade away. What kind of friend am I?"

"The best kind."

"You're grading on a curve."

"Yes, but you're always growing."

"The two people I hold most dear, after you of course, constantly travel. They're close but distant. I'm really comfortable with close but distant."

"Don't be too hard on yourself," she said.

"Did I choose Ransom because as PI and detective, we'll always be close but distant?"

"Calm down, Dr. Freud." She gave me another hug, then held me at arm's length with her hands on my arms. "You're not distant, El. You're right here where you're supposed to be."

With a nod of encouragement, she left me alone in the

room. Machines whirled and swooshed in tune with Lucy's breathing. I set my messenger bag next to her bed. I first pulled out the picture I pinched from her trailer, the one of her and her mom, and put it on the nightstand facing Lucy. I dragged a bulky recliner from the corner over to Lucy's bedside next to the pugs' booster.

"Let's talk, shall we?" I asked in a low voice, picking up Lucy's hand. "Sid is here for me and I am here for you. You are not alone. I'm sorry I was a terrible friend. I let my own life get in the way and it won't happen again." I squeezed her hand and thought about Lola and Lucy. Mother and daughter living in their trailer. Lola bringing us Kool-Aid while we played games on the astro grass. "I truly sincerely mean it. I'm here for you, so never ever think you're alone, okay?"

I took out my notebook and pen. "Where shall we start? The fairy tale characters? Yeah, can we talk about that? Are you being clever in your thinking or creating subterfuge should this book fall into the wrong hands? Or both? I'm thinking both." I pulled the lever on the side of the reclining chair to prop my feet up, startling the pugs. They yipped and I froze. Then we all settled back in.

"I assure you, dear Lucy, my hands are not the wrong hands. And I can certainly apply my own clever thinking to work this out. Let's align what I'm thinking with what I think you're thinking," I said softly. "That can't go wrong, right?"

I studied her notes, occasionally adding my own notes, then reorganized.

"Chas is Rumple. Your note says 'Track Wed.' Was this a tree you shook? He stays in play." I flipped to a new page. "Chef is Jiminy. Unless you meant Jessie is Jiminy and I cannot accept that you'd be so obvious when you clearly went to so much trouble to disguise. Unless that's your plan?"

The pugs snorfled and snored at my feet, no longer in their

booster, but rather sprawled on the vinyl floor. "I'm sticking with Chef as Jiminy. 'End scene' pretty much says it's safe to move him to the bottom. So for now, that's what I'm doing."

I turned the page. "Hook must be Austin, and you call him a genius with karma, and a follow up on Wednesday. Another tree? Why rocket man?" I made a note to listen to the Elton John song of the same name, see if there was something there. Kept him on the middle of the list.

"Red Riding Hood has to be Imogene the waitress. But what's the note about a deleted browser history? Were you poking around where you shouldn't?" I wish I knew when she wrote these notes. Before she shook trees or after. "Top of the list." After the year I'd had, it was no longer hard for me to believe someone would murder a friend. Unfortunately, statistics don't lie. Most murders really are committed by those closest to the victim.

"The Queen of Hearts and Geppetto. You've linked them together, looks like twice. Trading up, meaning a better man? I'm leaning strongly toward Bitsy, though Jane was dating Chef, so would she trade up? Jane was already pretty darn high up on the social ladder, assuming that's what 'ladder' meant, and had her own money. Bitsy makes more sense." I underlined Bitsy's name next to Queen of Hearts. But I had no idea who Geppetto was or where he ranked.

"You know, Lucy, seven is kind of a lot of viable suspects. Especially to harm your own mother. Could there really be that many people who wanted to hurt her?" I thought not.

The nurse slipped into the room to check her vitals and push buttons on the machines.

"How is she?" I asked.

"Good, really good," she said. "The doctor thinks she'll be able to come out of the coma in another few days. That's a good sign."

"Has she had many visitors? Friends? Family?" I asked.

"A few friends," she said. "Short supervised visits, of course."

"But no family?"

She raised a brow. "You mean her estranged father? That family?"

"That's the one."

"Not that I've seen."

She switched Lucy's IV bag, then quietly left.

I flipped through my pages. "Back to the Magnificent Seven. Though I've moved Chef off the list, so we're at the Hot Six. And last up is Granny. Tug Jensen or Grandma Virginia? You being literal or tricky? Or tricky being literal?" The note "too close" didn't help me any. Unless she meant Lola was too close, not Lucy. Because Lola was not close to Virginia, but definitely close to Tug. "I'm identifying Tug as Granny. Moving him to the bottom of the list." My thoughts from just a few minutes earlier danced in my head. Those closest to the victim can be the most dangerous. Tug was awfully close. And now he was running the entire operation. Moved him back to the middle.

I contemplated the asterisks beneath each name. "Is this a guilt-o-meter? The more stars, the more likely? Does a star represent the number of times you interviewed them or followed them?"

Realizing I hadn't accomplished much on my own, I added a new name to the bottom. Evil Queen. Threw in some stars and a name: Jane. Not a likely suspect, but she deserved to be on there someplace. Apparently she was very close to Chef and being quite secretive about it.

"Wait one minute, Miss Lucy Carmichael. Where is Jessie on your list? You specifically said you were here to prove him guilty." I paged through her seven suspects. None of her gibberishly outlined comments hinted at her dad other than the vague Jessie/Jiminy name connection. "Was that a red herring for me? You being tricky again? Could Rumpelstiltskin actually be Jessie and not Chas? Money as motive?"

I added one more line to my notes: Rumple: Jessie? Lucy said he was a sweet-talker, and Rumple certainly tricked people out of their money, and their lives, all the time.

Watching Lucy breathe, tapping my pen on the notebook, I couldn't help admire how far she'd come. She sussed out her suspects, created ciphers and codes, filled pages of notes, and likely identified the killer. It was a trip down the rabbit hole to follow her process, but she was really good at her job.

Her dangerous job.

A job I was four thousand training hours away from being qualified to do myself.

I slipped her mother's will out of my bag. "This document is awfully thin," I said, flipping through the pages.

Though written in legalese with lots of wheretos and heretofores, it was pretty easy to determine the gist. Fisher's Landing Trailer Park and Yacht Club reverted to former husband James Carmichael (as agreed to in the divorce decree, attached, marked Carmichael v. Carmichael). Lola's trailer and all personal belongings (including all bank accounts and safe deposit box contents) went to Lucille Carmichael. Custody of the two pugs, Colonel Mustard and Mrs. White, bestowed to Vivienne Ballantyne.

"What safe deposit box might that be, Lucy? Did your mom actually have one or was that a generic clause? What is your father going to do with the park now?" I continued to pose questions and Lucy continued to not answer them. She breathed softly in the quiet room. Her chest rose and fell in rhythm with the boxy machinery.

I sat with her another half an hour, telling her stories of my most interesting PI-in-training cases, like the case of the pilfered Pomeranians, and my most dangerous. In just one year I'd tackled the murder of a board member, a stolen Fabergé Egg which also led to murder, and the poisoning of a young ballerina.

I once told Lucy (when she still lived on the island) that performing discreet inquiries for Ballantyne patrons was no more difficult than solving a middle grade mystery. Gather the clues, work the case. Fourth grade logic worked pretty much every time. I'd never been proven wrong. Yet, anyway.

As the time closed in on eleven p.m., I packed up my bag and the pugs.

There were no pugs.

I hadn't even noticed their snoring rumbles had stopped.

In two seconds, I was on hands and knees, scouring the floor. Beneath the bed, behind the rolling machinery, beyond the squat nightstand-like table.

Oh my God. The recliner. I flipped the lever. The bottom flew up. I shoved my hands under the fabric flap. Metal parts, a base. I slapped the floor, nearly upended the chair. No pugs.

I started to sweat.

How did they disappear? The beef sticks abandoned, the booster empty. I'd never moved from my spot.

But the nurse came in.

I flung open the door, which did not fling. It slowly whooshed opened. I peeked into the hallway. The officer assigned to the door gave me a head nod and returned to staring straight ahead.

It was late, quiet, and there were dozens upon dozens of rooms with hallways leading every which way.

"They escaped about an hour and a half ago," the nurse said to me. She stood about three doors down and waved.

I rushed over to her and she put her finger to her lips.

"They're fine," she said softly. "I've been going room to room with them, cheering patients. But you have to see this."

An elderly woman slept in a bed like Lucy's. Soft rhythmic machines whirred in the background. Colonel Mustard and Mrs. White were snuggled in the crook of her arm. Their snores mixed with hers.

"She hasn't had a single visitor in the three weeks she's been here," the nurse said. "First time I seen her smile. And first time she's fallen asleep before two a.m."

I wanted to leave them there all night. All week. Forever. This sweet little woman, frail arms, wispy white hair, cuddled with puppies, was a radiant spot in a dreadful week.

The nurse gently lifted the pugs from the bed. "You go on home," she said. "But don't be afraid to bring them back."

"Thank you," I said. "I don't even know your name."

She lifted the credentials on her long lanyard to show me. "Marjorie Thistle."

"Thank you, Marjorie. I appreciate all you've done."

We took the puppies back to Lucy's room and I packed everything up. With a squeeze of Lucy's hand, I reassured her one more time.

"I'll figure this out, Lucy. The killer won't get away. I promise."

FIFTEEN

(Day #6: Thursday Morning)

Another morning, another trip down the beach with crazy barking mini dogs. Just putting this out there: I did not understand how folks with children and pets got anything done. My life's motto has been that I do what I want. Within the confines of running a billion-dollar charity, hosting large parties, and helping patrons out of minor jams. Other than that, I do what I want. Not so much with two dogs strapped to my chest. Granted, others may not worry their puppies will be kidnapped and held for ransom. But what do I know? Maybe they did.

Once all paws were sufficiently rinsed and towel-dried, I showered while they gobbled, then tucked them into the Mini. I skipped my own meal and went straight to the Big House for a board meeting and a gourmet mouth-watering breakfast that would make my Honey Nut Cheerios float with envy.

We zipped around Oyster Cove and up the Big House drive. I unloaded the pug twins, taking more time than a family of five at the mall trying to load wiggly babies into a complicated eight-wheeled stroller. Note to self: I bet someone made a dog stroller.

I hooked leashes to collars and we trotted through the foyer to the parlor where Carla had set out a spread worthy of a Cheerio's envy. Breakfast empanadas stuffed with fluffy eggs and cheddar, frosted Mexican pastries, fresh squeezed mango juice smoothies, and bowls of colorful cut fruit decorated the entire side credenza.

Board members oohed and aahed over the cutest puppies ever to grace the United States as I grabbed an empty china plate.

"Elliott, I need to see you," Jane snapped from the doorway. With a full spin, she left the room.

"Of course," I said and set my plate back. I walked out the door and nearly knocked her over. "Oh, right here, you mean."

"Where else?" Jane said. "Don't answer. Just tell me what's—wait. Why are there dogs?"

"Puppies. This is Colonel Mustard and Mrs. White."

"For the love of Jesus in a jumpsuit."

I pushed the button on the leash box instead of clicking it, and the pair happily stretched the cord to its limits. They promptly pawed at Jane's legs. With scratchy puppy nails.

"Before you lose it, these adorable dogs are Vivi's. Lola's first, now Vivi's, and they were kidnapped yesterday." I quickly told her our harrowing tale and she looked unimpressed.

"Fine. But keep them on your side of this conversation."

I untangled them, winding them around her legs, then my legs, then zipped the leashes to a shorter length. "Continue," I said.

"What's going on with Chef?"

"I need to talk to him."

"We've been over that already. The answer is no. What else?"

"The answer can't be no. Chef Newhouse was sniffing around the Wharf this week. Gossip is spreading and the vultures are circling. I don't think Chef is in a position to ignore me."

"This isn't about you."

"I know that. But I need to know what he knows. What happened that day? I need to hear it from him. How did he end up with his hand on a knife in Lola's chest? What happened?"

"He found her like that. End of story. He's already said what he's going to say, so figure the rest out."

"Wait, you're talking to him? How do you know he found her like that?"

"Of course I'm talking to him," Jane said.

"Then he needs to let me talk to him," I said. "He has inside information. He knows more than he thinks he knows. Time is moving quickly and he needs to talk to me."

"I'm not going against his wishes."

"He wishes to be convicted of murder."

"Then you need to work faster before that happens."

"Good Lord in Heaven, why won't you help me?"

"Help you? This is your job. If you'd do it for once, then it wouldn't matter what Chef says."

"For once? I have helped you out of a jam, serious-murder-suspect jams, more than once—"

"It was only once, Sherlock."

"You need to trust me," I said. "I know what needs to be done."

"Trust you?" Jane said with a harsh laugh.

"Set up a meeting with Chef!" I said. I may have yelled.

Jane yanked me two feet away from the parlor door. "This is confidential. Meaning no blabbing to anyone. Not your partner in crime, Sid Bassi, nor your life partner, Lieutenant what's his name."

"I'll hold your confidence, I promise," I said. "You can trust me."

She looked away, then back at me. "Fine, I trust you."

"Tell that to your face."

"You want to hear this or not?" She blew out a deep breath.

"Jessie was a decent kid, but always in trouble. Dumb trouble. Stealing pumpkins on Halloween, joyriding his neighbor's car. He once spray-painted his name on the school wall. But Tom adored him. Jessie was the cool one, the bad boy. Tom was the teacher's pet. Nerdy, straight A's, and relentlessly picked on."

"Kids can be cruel."

"I meant in his family. Mother, father, cousins. You've met Virginia. She seem like the type to appreciate a distinguished chef?"

"So Tom wanted to fit in and decided to confess to murder?"

"Tom was accepted to the finest culinary school in Europe. He'd train under the best. His senior year. Jessie took him out one night to celebrate, but the police caught them stealing a car in downtown Savannah. Jessie covered for Tom. Let him run while Jessie took the blame. That fall, Jessie went to jail, Tom went to Paris."

The pugs grew tired of all this standing still. They yanked the leash, cried, pawed at my legs, scratched the wall, nipped each other.

"Tom's family never accepted him," Jane said. "Too good for them, if you ask me. But he loves them. He loves Jessie and feels he owes him. Owes him his entire career, which has been his whole life."

"But still, the death penalty?"

"Gregory Mead will get that off the table. In the meantime, you need to find another way out. Tom absolutely did not kill Lola. We both know it. You're supposed to be getting your investigator license. So go investigate."

Zibby Archibald stuck her head out of the doorway. She wore what could only be described as a tam o'shanter: a green and white plaid hat with a pom pom plopped on top. "The golf tournament's already teed up and sailing down the green.

Should we shelve the meeting?"

"Absolutely not," Jane said. "I'm finished here."

"Is this the Captain and Mrs. Tennille?" Zibby asked. She knelt to pug height and they gave her lovin' while she sang to them. *"Don't go breakin' my heart."*

"I think that's Elton John and Kiki Dee," I said.

"I'm embarrassed for you that you know that," Jane said.

"Love will keep us together," I said to Zibby.

"Yes it will, dear," Zibby said. She patted my hand and deftly took the leashes from me, following Jane back into the parlor.

I remained outside the door as board members streamed in, all wearing various forms of golf attire. From knickers to khakis to some sort of kilt. Most of us were heading to Vista Lakes after today's meeting for the annual tournament benefitting the Summerton Coalition for Youth Sports. With the Ballantyne's involvement, participation was not optional, but arriving at lunch made perfect timing. I would never actually play in the tournament. I'm not athletic. Not that I needed to be crossfit-ready to play golf, but my bike had three wheels and a basket, if that helped explain my athletic capacity.

Matty touched my arm, gently pulling me farther from the door. "You have a second?"

"Of course, how's Lucy?" I asked.

"I was going to ask you," he said. "She's the same. I saw her this morning. You?"

"Last night. I'm sorry, Matty." I reached for his hand. It was soft and tan and felt familiar. "She'll be okay."

"Yeah, I think so."

Ransom passed by us. I suddenly felt very aware of Matty's hand in mine. Ransom wasn't in the parlor one minute before he came out with Jane. They didn't even look our way. Headed straight toward her office.

"Did Lucy say anything to you?" I asked. "Anything at all?"

"About her mother's death?" Matty said.

"Or her investigation? Or who she'd been talking to? Really, anything at all." When he didn't answer after a full twenty seconds, I added, "I can help."

"I know, but I just don't know anything." He looked stressed: tense shoulders, furrowed brow. But then smiled a small smile. "I can't escape the allure, I guess."

"The allure?" I asked.

"Of the kick-ass investigator." He squeezed my hand. "I have a type, apparently."

"Did you just call me kick-ass?"

He laughed and we went inside the parlor.

I grabbed a plate just as Jane walked in. I excused myself from Matty and approached her. "What did Ransom say to you?"

"It was private," Jane said and breezed by me.

Virginia Carmichael entered the room chin first. She made direct eye contact with nearly every board member before zeroing in on me. "You think you're all this." She approached at a steady pace. She stopped barely two feet from me, pointing a finger straight at my face. "You stole from my granddaughter. You are a thief."

Ransom walked in behind her, standing to the side, while the entirety of the board stood in various positions behind me. Some eating, some seated, and all of them focused on the hullabaloo about to go down. I felt their intensity more than saw it. My body temperature rose ten degrees.

"I am not a thief, Mrs. Carmichael," I said. "I would never steal from Lucy."

"Really? Then where are her keys and phone?"

"I have no idea," I said slowly. I casually set my plate on the table, taking the opportunity to take a step back.

Virginia squinted at me. "You don't own that hospital staff. At least not all of them. I'll get those possessions back and you'll not get away with this. With any of it."

"Mrs. Carmichael? I'm Lieutenant Ransom with the Sea Pine Police Department. Perhaps I could help?"

"The lieutenant who arrested my son? My son who now sits in jail awaiting the death penalty?"

"Your son who confessed."

"Stop meddling in my business," Virginia said with a hard stare at me. She once-overed Ransom, then left.

The exchange took less time than I spent brushing my teeth, but it still rattled me.

"We should talk," Ransom said.

"I have the board meeting," I said.

"We can certainly run it without you," Jane said, adding as Ransom and I left the room, "We can run this whole operation without you."

I ignored her, but it stung. In one sentence, she hit on my fear the Foundation didn't need me. Or worse. I'd become a liability, not an asset.

I kept my rattled core and exposed fears tucked deep inside as we settled in my office. Me behind the desk, Ransom in a visitor's chair, and a nine-gallon jug of hand-sani a barrier between us.

"Did you take—" Ransom cleared his throat. "Did you borrow Lucy's keys and phone from the hospital?"

"What did you talk to Jane about? Chef Carmichael? A new development in the case?"

"This case is closed."

"Officially? If I called the captain, he'd also say it's closed?"

"He'd say we share information. You, the Ballantyne's PI-in-training, with the Sea Pine Police. As part of your sponsorship, to keep your pursuit of a valid PI license in good standing, cooperation is essential. He'd also ask about Lucy's keys and phone."

I took a pump from the hand-sani well.

"In the spirit of cooperation," Ransom said.

"In the spirit of cooperation, you're telling me Chef confessed, case closed. Not sure what I'm cooperating with."

Crickets.

"I was only asking about Jane, the Foundation's board chair," I said. "As major supporters of the Sea Pine Island Police Department, Edward and Vivi Ballantyne entrust me to stay apprised of things. As for the keys, I'm sure they are at the hospital or in the care of a long-time trusted friend."

"And the phone?"

"If I had to guess? Probably not at the hospital when Lucy was brought in. Likely missing. Presumed to have been taken by her attacker."

We sat in the quiet of my office. Him staring at me, me staring back.

"If there's nothing else?" I said.

"There's nothing else."

"Nothing you or the police department want to share with me?"

Silence.

"I must get back to the meeting," I said. "Who knows what Jane is doing in there."

He stood and held his arm out in an "after you" type gesture.

With an impersonal head tip, we went our separate ways. Ransom walked out the front door and I went into the parlor.

The empty parlor.

Zibby was wobbling her way out when I walked in, the pugs skipping along next to her.

"Hey Zibby, where is everyone?"

"Jane adjourned us," she said. Her tam was askew and the tail end of a dinner napkin stuck out from her blazer sleeve. "Time to hit the links! Jane said we'd re-meeting next week."

A single pink-frosted pastry sat on the credenza. The rest of the spread was picked over and depleted. Not being a pastry snob, I gladly plopped it on a plate and sat at the table alone. I knew the same spread was over at the ninth hole, probably larger with twice the food options. But I needed a hit of pure sugar to fortify me. I scarfed that sucker in three ravenous bites, saving two nibbles for my curly-tailed companions. I'd already had encounters with Jane, Ransom, and Virginia Carmichael. And my day was just getting started.

"*Ballantyne Director Grilled by Lover,*" Tate said from the doorway. "Catchy headline, right?"

"Lover?" I said.

"I was going to say Lieutenant Lover, but it sounds too tabloidy." He poured himself a cup of coffee from the silver urn at the end of the credenza.

"The lieutenant didn't grill me," I said. "You know full well I work closely with the Sea Pine police."

"Which is why I added lover."

"What can I do for you, Tate?"

"You can tell me why you're investigating a murder someone already confessed to. Why the Sea Pine lieutenant who arrested him is actively conducting an investigation here at the Big House. How the Ballantyne Foundation let a murderer—"

"Stop. I meant to say 'no comment.'"

Tate leaned his arms on the top of the tall chair opposite me. "I scratch your back, you scratch mine."

My face scrunched in disdain at the visual.

He chuckled. "You help me with my article. Provide essential details. An off-the-record source close to the investigation, if you like."

"And in return?"

"I won't use lover in the headline."

"Sounds fair." I rose and brushed crumbs from my hands. Carried my plate to the sideboard.

"Fantastic," he said. "I'll follow you to the—"

"That was sarcasm, Tate. I don't care what you call Lieutenant Ransom. But I do care how you frame the Ballantyne. A single word of slander or libel, and I'll make sure the next thing you write is a big fat check to one of our charities after you've been fired from the *Islander Post*."

With a pat to my thigh, the pugs and I marched from the parlor. It was too late for Tate to make today's edition. That meant his story was slated for Sunday. I couldn't stop him from running it, but I still had time to change the story before it printed.

SIXTEEN

(Day #6: Thursday Afternoon)

The Vista Lakes Country Club was a private golf community about halfway between the Palmetto Bridge and Savannah. I drove down the long winding entrance road lined with fake gas lamps and a stone wall. The entire place resembled the more expensive Poplar Grove, about five miles north on the May River, only not quite as fancy. Their roads were trimmed in brick, their walls accented with climbing wisteria.

I registered at the gate, giving the guard my name. Once a paper pass had been placed in my windshield, I continued down the lane until I reached the two-story clubhouse, restaurant, and pro shop.

Golfers milled around the lobby in clusters, most with drinks in their hands, spilling out from the club restaurant and bar overlooking the eighteenth hole. I followed the chitter chatter to the back deck, daring anyone to stop me and my pint-sized entourage. They didn't. Apparently pampered pets were welcome all over the establishment. Miniature dogs in breeds ranging from curly-haired to long-nosed danced around fancy shoes and designer handbags. I kept the pugs' leash boxes clutched tight in my hands. If someone tried to take them, they were taking me, too.

We paused at the gorgeous lunch display spread out on four

buffet tables including ones with fruity drinks and luscious desserts, all to greet golfers as they exited the final hole, their tournament play complete. The Ballantyne used to sponsor the eighteenth hole, but hosting was an all-day affair. With the Irish Spring the same week, I could only do so much. Now we sponsor the ninth hole, the halfway point. This year Carla set up a tent: early birds got mango mimosas, egg and chorizo burritos, and breakfast empanadas, all with her homemade guacamole and fresh red pepper salsa. The afternoon crowd got carne asada quesadillas and pulled pork empanadas with mango margaritas. She manned the affair with an oversized grill and plenty of staff and it was going to be my first stop.

Austin Metwally must have snuck a locator beacon in my shoe because he approached me before I said hello to a single soul.

"Miss Elliott, so great you made it." He wore full caddy garb: polo shirt, cargo shorts, and some kind of tournament bib with enormous pockets across the front. "You're going to love my plans. You and the Ballantyne. I've got a brochure here..." He dug into his pouches.

"I'm sure it's—"

"Here we go." He whipped out a wrinkled pamphlet with writing in all the margins. "It's the nine-hole off Cabana in Summerton. You know, over by the Target center? Been nearly abandoned a year now. Bank owns it, and I'm putting in an offer. When they see my plans, I'll be a shoo-in. It's going to be something special. We're going to have themed-holes."

"Themed holes?"

"Like miniature golf, but professional. I've got a call in with Jack Nicklaus to sponsor. He's already got five courses he's designed here in the county. Must be his favorite place, so why not one more?"

"Jack Nicklaus is interested?"

"He will be when I get him out here to see what I'm talking about. He might even want to co-own it." He handed me a business card and two more brochures.

I tucked them away and made my excuses. Mostly to go eat. Carla's spread could wait, my grumbling stomach could not, especially with twenty-five feet of brunch within reach. I grabbed a plate from a tall stack on a table at one end. I normally avoid buffets the way one might avoid eating food from a table made from toxic waste barrels covered in asbestos. People sneeze and cough and breathe all over those buffet bowls of community chow, carelessly touching and picking with their germy fingers. But I made exceptions when in polite society. And when I was starving.

I mostly chose fruit from the bottom of the bowl and frequented the chef stations where they prepared fluffy frittatas and silky crepes to order. I grabbed a high top table near the railing and hoisted myself onto the barstool just as I noticed a large architectural drawing to my immediate left. I first thought the drawing was of Vista Lakes, the country club where I was dining, but it wasn't. It only looked similar. And the name was slightly different. Island Vista, not Vista Lakes. Drawn right in the corner of this new Island Vista development: Tug Boat Slim's.

Upon closer inspection, with my nose nearly pressed to the foam core and my jaw clenched so it wouldn't drop in the most unladylike way, I studied the plans for a brand new luxury condo community with a yacht club. On Lola Carmichael's property.

Several brochures were stacked in an attached plastic holder. It looked like one of the brochures from Lola's trailer. I'd only glanced at them and later assumed they were all for Chas's development across the way, the Palmetto Bay Sailing Club. Obviously I'm a terrible investigator. Or at least I was on this case. I completely overlooked that the brochures weren't all from the same development. Maybe one of them was also from Austin? I didn't even check. I needed to get out of my head and into this investigation.

"You interested in the finest condominium community Sea Pine Island's ever seen?" A boisterous man dressed in standard country club attire (logo'd polo, fine slacks, leather belt not quite holding it all together) said, tapping the board as he spoke. "Unsurpassed views, private club access. It's a beauty." He held out his hand. "Hollis Jones. I own Vista Lakes, so that makes me your tournament host."

"I'm Elliott Lisbon," I said and shook his hand. "With the Ballantyne Foundation."

"Really now. How nice to finally meet you. I know you been working with my staff for these functions. I'm sorry Edward Ballantyne couldn't make it."

"He sends his regrets."

"I'll make a note to reach out to him. Set up an exclusive tour of Island Vista for your board members and wealthier patrons. This development will sell out right quick. You mark my words."

"This is Lola Carmichael's land," I said.

"Well, it was," he said. "God rest her soul. We were in final negotiations. She was real excited about it."

Chas and Bitsy Obermeyer joined us in the corner of the restaurant deck. Chas's chest was puffed out and his face was cardinal red. "You're such a liar. Lola wasn't selling you her park and you damn well know it."

"Elliott, nice to see you," Bitsy said. "What in the world? Are those dogs?"

"They're Vivi's," I said.

"They're adorable," Bitsy said. "Are Vivi and Edward home?"

"That little boat park you're building is going to be in trouble when my five-star yacht club breaks ground," Hollis said.

"It'll never happen," Chas said.

"Sooner than you think," Hollis said. "You can put up roadblocks, but I'm from Florida, and we bulldoze over roadblocks. Developing waterfront is in my genes." He turned to me. "Let's get that special tour set up before there's nothing left to buy." He tipped his head toward Bitsy and walked away.

"Elliott, you didn't answer my question," Bitsy said. "Are Edward and Vivi home yet? Didn't you say this week? We have the Oglevie dinner party tonight."

"Friday," I said. "They return Friday."

"Hey Mr. Obermeyer," Austin said. "Did you see the plans for my new nine-hole course? I'm in talks with Jack Nicklaus."

"Oh hell," Chas said. "Jack Nicklaus is not investing in a nine-hole."

I spotted Deidre on the far side of the deck. "If you'll excuse me, I see I'm needed over there." I waved at no one in particular and scurried away.

"Over where?" Bitsy said, but I just walked faster.

"You made it," Deidre said. "Pretty nice spread. Though Carla's is nicer."

"Oh!" I said. "My lunch." I watched as a server in a black bowtie picked up my untouched plate and stacked it with the others in her hand, clearing the tables along the rail.

"How's the investigation?" Deidre said, leaning in close. "Who's your biggest suspect?"

"No one has risen to the top of the list," I said. "But I need to eat before I faint flat out, smack my head on this wood deck, and bleed to death."

"I'm always up for seconds," Deidre said.

I created an identical lunch plate to my first, while Deidre created hers with items from the buffet bowls. We sat at a table near the lemonade jugs. Deidre kindly set down a dish of water next to the pugs lounging on the deck.

"I saw a Mahjong set at Lola's," I said and took my first bite. Melted cheddar, fresh spinach, fluffy eggs. I took another before finishing my thought. "Did you ever see Lola play?"

"No, not in our club league," Deidre said. "Though our crowd is intimidating and the waiting list is three years long. But there have to be a dozen Mahj groups on the island."

"It's probably nothing. Her set didn't look like it got much use."

"Maybe the entertainment center at the park? I'm sure they play board games over there. I bet Jessie knows. You should ask him." Deidre looked around.

"He's here?"

"Sure, I saw him talking to Chas earlier."

"When?" I said, scoping out the restaurant. I stood to see over the rail and down to the path around the eighteenth hole.

"Not long, maybe fifteen minutes before I saw you."

"I have got to find that man." I grabbed my bag, and with a pat to Deidre's shoulder, walked down the steps. The leash handles secured to the chair yanked me back as my feet tangled in the black cords.

"You go on, sweetie," she said to me. "I've been dying to have these two all to myself."

"You really don't mind?" I asked, descending two more steps.

"Not one little bit."

Before she could change her mind, I skipped down the remaining three steps to the mingling golfers on the perfectly cut green grass.

I didn't see Jessie, but I saw Hollis Jones, owner of that very green grass, talking with Bitsy Obermeyer. She smiled.

Placed her hand on his arm, like a playful touch. He leaned in close, said something in her ear. She laughed, then walked toward the eighteenth hole while he continued on the path toward a coordinating side building. It looked like a miniature clubhouse. Same architecture, same design.

Following the curvy brick paver path, I pulled open a wood door tall enough to accommodate Kareem Abdul-Jabbar. A metal plate affixed to the side said: Vista Builders, est. 1985.

The lobby entrance was dressed in tufted armchairs and overstuffed sofas. Polished marble floors gleamed beneath ornate rugs. Pale yellow walls with stacked white trim showcased arched windows overlooking the golf course.

"Hello?" I heard shuffling in an office toward the back where the lights popped on. "Mr. Jones?"

"Yes?" he said, then walked out to meet me. "Miss Lisbon, how nice to see you."

"Do you have a minute to talk?"

"Of course. Come in, come in."

He ushered me to a large space in the corner of his office to a pool-table-like diorama, just like the one at Chas's development. The Island Vista logo flew on tiny flags near the entrance. Gone was Fisher's Landing Trailer Park and Yacht Club. Lola's trailer, the entertainment center, the short pier near Tug Boat Slim's, all gone.

"It's a beaut, am I right?" Hollis pointed out the different buildings, walking trails, an elaborate gated entrance.

"It's lovely," I said. "But I'm confused. Lola loved Fisher's Landing. I can't imagine her ever wanting to leave."

"Well, she's a funny thing," he said. "She really did love that junkyard. A pip, that one. But now Jessie, her husband, he knows a good deal. We'll get it wrapped up lickety-split."

"After probate, you mean."

"Yeah, yeah. Sorry for the loss. May she rest in peace."

"Is Vista Lakes your first development?"

"Hell no. I got seven condo communities in Florida from Boca Raton right on down to Coral Gables. Building's in my blood. My father was a builder, now me. Someday, my son."

Well, hello, Geppetto. Not quite a woodworking handyman, but I thought builder was certainly close enough. I was looking at Suspect #6.

While part of me celebrated identifying another suspect, I casually took two steps toward the door, keeping his desk solidly between us, wondering if anyone else was in the quiet offices. He was a suspect for a reason. "Were you upset when Lola wouldn't sell?" I asked.

He laughed. "Look little lady, she'd have come around. We were just getting started."

"Seems as if you are pretty far into this project," I said with a wave at the diorama. "From the looks of it, you have a lot of money invested into a property you don't own. One that's not even under contract."

His smile stayed in place but the good humor in his tone faded. "Everyone has their price. Even Lola Carmichael."

I slowly nodded and glanced at the brochures on his desk and noticed a handful of business cards. Recent visitors? One had the Sea Pine Police Department logo. Lieutenant Nick Ransom.

"Lieutenant Ransom came by?" He sure did make the rounds for someone who had a closed case.

Hollis stepped forward. "What exactly do you do for the Ballantyne Foundation?"

"Director."

"Like I said, I'm happy to set up a private presentation for Edward and your wealthier patrons." He took one more step toward me. "Anything else?"

"Thank you for your time. I appreciate it." I reached down

for one of the thick brochure folders. "May I?"

"Of course," he said. "Take two."

With the glossy packet in my hand, I left the mini clubhouse building. Making my way back to the tournament, another block fell into place. Might be a leap, but with that intimate exchange on the sidewalk, did that make Bitsy the Queen of Hearts to his Geppetto? Lucy's notation said they'd met. It even questioned if Bitsy was trading up or trading secrets. Geppetto and Rumple were development rivals. I wondered how serious a suspect Hollis Jones was. He made a point. Most everyone had a price, and he seemed as if he had the money to pay it.

SEVENTEEN

(Day #6: Thursday Late Afternoon)

Once free of the clubhouse offices, I snagged a golf cart and the pugs and zipped my way straight to the ninth hole respite station. Wind blew their ears back and I felt as if I was doing a public service. With all the driving around, I was making them puppies who didn't get motion sick and who could behave whilst in motion. Only they didn't behave that well.

Though I'd just dined on a lovely frittata brunch, I thought it would be rude to not at least sample some of Carla's spread. She packed me a basket for my golf cart, and with the pugs secured in their booster in the passenger seat, we spent the entire afternoon noshing and searching for one Jessie Carmichael. Like looking for Bigfoot. I wasn't convinced he existed.

Three false alarms and I finally left the golf course to search the island. Up and down the length of Cabana Boulevard twice, passing Charter Bank each time. On the third pass, my brain finally started working. Chas was at the golf tournament, which meant he was not at the bank. I didn't need a warrant to find out who paid off Lola's mortgage. I needed ambrosia salad.

My tiny dashboard clock said 3:55. I slapped the gas pedal and raced my ice blue convertible driving machine to the Big House, slowing only to wait for the gate bar to lift at Oyster

Cove.

I whipped up the drive and parked right out front. The Ballantyne Foundation offices were quiet with only minimal staff tending to the grounds and interior. The kitchen was empty. Low lights illuminated the counters. I opened the enormous stainless steel refrigerator door and raided its contents.

No ambrosia salad, no pretzel salad. Probably better that way. I didn't want to compete with Lola's memory. I peered around covered containers, fresh veggies and homemade dressings, and food-making things like eggs and cream and bottles I didn't recognize. What I did recognize? A whole fruit tart with a shiny glaze and crisp crust. I carefully boxed it, tied it with string, and secured it in the backseat.

Fifteen minutes later, I carried my package into Charter Bank, not stopping until I placed it with flourish on Chas's secretary's desk.

"What's this?" Ann asked, a glance first at the bakery box, then at the toy team at our feet.

I ignored the dogs. It was starting to get easier. "For you," I said, sitting in the chair next to her desk. "Can we talk?"

"Of course. Though I may not be who you need." She looked around. "I think we still have an accounts manager here."

"You're exactly who I need, Ann," I said. "I am here on behalf of Lola Carmichael."

She stopped looking around after a sideways peek at Chas's closed door.

"First, something easy," I said.

"Okay."

"Did Lola have a safe deposit box here?"

Ann shifted in her seat. "Not so easy. That's confidential."

"I understand," I said. "I'm not asking for the contents. Only whether or not she had one at this bank."

Uncomfortable seconds ticked by, but I kept my lips padlocked tight to wait her out.

"I suppose it can't hurt," she finally said. "Yes and no. She had one reserved, but she, um, passed before she could use it."

"Thank you, Ann. Now, what I'm going to tell you next is private," I said, lowering my voice, even though there wasn't a person within twenty feet of us. "Lola Carmichael was financially strapped, nearing foreclosure on her property. Likely headed for a quick bankruptcy."

"I know," Ann said. "It was awful. I felt so bad for her."

"But one day, out of nowhere, without warning, someone, some decent human being, saved her home and her business. Paid her late balance in full."

"I know," Ann said. "I was so happy for her."

My top secret confidential conversation was nothing more than recapping what Ann already knew. Was nothing private on this island? "Lola tasked me to find out the identity of this benefactor."

"Uh-huh." Ann leaned back in her chair. It rolled an inch away from me.

"Lola was distraught. She knew something was wrong. She needed answers." I pulled Lola's handwritten note from my bag and set it in front of Ann. "She gave me authorization to investigate only hours before she died."

Ann ran her hand over the note, smoothing out a crinkled corner.

"She was my friend," I said. "I have to help her. This is important."

"How do you know it's important? It might not be related."

"Absolutely true. But I won't know until I have all the information. Information you can give me."

"I don't have the authority to open Chas's client's accounts." She tapped on her keyboard with one hand, then shut off her monitor. "When he's not here. Without his permission. It's against the rules unless he's made an exception. If you need me to look at Lola's account, I can't."

I picked up Lola's note and slipped it back in my bag. "I understand. I don't want you to get into trouble."

Ann looked torn. She bit her lip and clenched her hands together on top of her desk.

"May I ask one more question? Then I'll be on my way."

"Of course."

"Do you need to look into Lola's account to tell me who paid the balance?"

She stared at me, not breaking eye contact. I heard the tellers at the counter rattle keys as a clock somewhere in the room chimed. Closing time.

"I'm locking up," a woman said. "You staying late, Ann?"

Ann unclenched her hands and smoothed her skirt, then reached into a drawer and pulled out her handbag. "We're done. Just wrapped up." She stood and picked up the bakery box I'd left on her desk. "And this?"

"I couldn't come empty-handed," I said, grabbing my own keys out of my shorty pants pocket. "Lola would've been mortified. It was her way."

Ann nodded slowly. With her handbag on her shoulder and the box in her hand, she tucked in her chair. She leaned closer and said something softly as she passed me on her way out the door. "The anonymous benefactor? Chas Obermeyer."

I dropped my keys and startled the pugs. I stared as Ann walked out the glass doors, the puppies engrossed in my tassel keychain at my feet.

"That little shit," I whispered. That was my first thought. My second: Why did he secretly pay off the mortgage on Fisher's Landing?

The last remaining bank teller held the door while I

untangled the pugs from around my ankles. We then marched straight to the Mini. Colonel Mustard and Mrs. White were as steamed as I was, even though they didn't know why. By the time I drove over to the Palmetto Bay Sailing Club trailer, hitting every green light except the one red one that was nearly orange so it was okay to blast through, they were closed. Not sure if Chas or Bitsy would've stopped by their sales trailer after the golf tournament, but certainly worth the ten-minute drive to find out. I may have missed him tonight, but I knew how to hunt him down tomorrow.

While I was in the neighborhood, I went to Fisher's Landing to find Jessie Carmichael. I felt like a stalker driving the aisles of the trailer park at random intervals. I finally gave up around feeding time. I had just passed through the gates at Oyster Cove when my phone rang.

"Hey Elli," Deidre said. "You up for dinner? You should come to Ida Claire's for tonight's special. It's very special."

"I'm nearly at my cottage. Cereal over the sink awaits me." Barely a bowl, really. Maybe I should order a pizza. My earlier adrenaline had seeped out and a big carb pie sounded divine.

"That doesn't sound nearly as good as Ida Claire's," Deidre said. "You should really, really consider the special."

"I hear you, nothing beats their chicken and waffles," I said. "Don't tell Carla I said that."

Deidre lowered her voice. "I'm speaking in code, Elli. Jessie Carmichael is eating dinner here right now. *That* dinner special."

I hit the brakes, swerved the Mini Coop around a palm tree island halfway to my cottage, then zoomed right back out the Oyster Cove gates with a fresh burst of adrenaline. "On my way. Where are you? Can you watch the pugs?"

"I'm sorry, Elli, but I'm still here at the diner. We're in the same boat. And I'm headed to a library event right after."

"What am I supposed to do with them? I can't take them inside. It's like summer in the everglades in that diner."

"Don't I know it," she said.

It took twelve minutes to skedaddle my way to Ida Claire's on Marsh Land Road. I passed a beat-up Winnebago parked about fifty feet down from the entrance. Its nose pointed at me, away from Ida Claire's.

The lot was full, so I wedged the Mini Coop between a pickup truck and the sidewalk, though my tires might have been fully on the sidewalk.

The watchcat at the door went insane upon sniffing two dogs. I'd bundled them in the booster seat and hoisted them in front of me. If I had locked them in the leather carrier, they would have fainted from heat exhaustion before we sat down.

A wall of boggy hot air greeted me. People jammed the tables, and there wasn't an empty barstool at the counter, either. Looked like locals, mostly because I recognized nearly everyone. I waved at Deidre in the corner dining with two board members and spotted Austin and Imogene as I walked through the restaurant.

"You given any thought to my proposal?" Austin asked.

"Not yet, but I will," I said.

"And Lucy?" he asked. "Only got to see her for five minutes. I sent flowers, though. Maybe I should've sent more?"

"She's doing better," I said. "Flowers are perfect. She'll love them."

He started to stand, but I patted his shoulder and kept on moving. I'd spotted Jessie, the same man who'd driven the Winnebago out of Fisher's Landing, sitting in a middle booth with a plate of fried chicken and waffles nearly polished off.

"Jessie Carmichael?" I started to slide into the vinyl booth across from him but he jumped up mid-sit.

"Elli Lisbon," he said with arms open wide. He hugged me

as if we were bffs, long lost friends, childhood sweethearts, squishing the box of dogs between us.

I swear to all things holy, I'd never met this man in all my life. "Nice to see you, Jessie," I said, hugging back. "I'm so sorry about Lola. She was adored at the Ballantyne."

"She was adored by everyone," Jessie said. "Woman was an angel." He gestured to the booth seat. "Sit, sit. What can I do you for? You here for me or for the chicken?"

I eyeballed his dinner and looked around for the server. Not going to lie, I love my cereal, but let's get real. I was not passing this dinner up.

A woman dressed like Imogene (slash Alice), sashayed over and took my order. She brought a slushy Pepsi and refilled Jessie's iced tea. She only briefly glimpsed at Colonel Mustard and Mrs. White chomping Bullies in the booster wedged in beside me. I was beginning to think people hauled their dogs everywhere on this island and I'd never noticed.

"How you been?" Jessie asked.

"Been good, been good," I said. "Except—"

"These Lola's new babies? Attorney said she had a pair of pugs." He reached a finger across the table, letting Mrs. White lick syrup from it.

"Yes, these were her babies."

"You always carry them around? Thought they was for Vivi."

I watched him carefully, checking for sincerity or skullduggery. "I don't like leaving them alone. Even with the new impenetrable security system in my cottage and the overprotective police lieutenant who lives next door."

"Sounds like you're guarding the queen's castle instead of a cottage."

"Somedays it feels that way."

"That's the truth," he said. "It's been a helluva week. First

Lola, then my brother."

"I didn't realize you and Chef were so close."

"Yeah, seems so."

I leaned across the table, co-conspirator to co-conspirator. "Is he covering for you?"

"Be the first time. And you know what they say, first time for everything and better late than never."

"So you admit it? He's taking the fall?"

"Hell, no—"

Jessie cut off as the waitress plopped my dinner next to my soda cup. The honeyed scents of fresh fried chicken swirled toward the pugs and I pushed my plate out of smelling distance. They nearly jumped free. I think out of smelling distance might be about a mile down the road. I smeared a smidge of tangy dipping sauce in the middle of their Bully where they had not yet chewed and they vowed to love me forever.

"You supposed to do that?" he asked.

"I have no idea," I said. "I only know about chocolate and poinsettias being dangerous for dogs." I soaked more hand-sani into my palms and fingertips, nearly running through my third full bottle in a single day. I would wash my hands, but would then also have to take the dogs with me. A vicious cycle. "You were saying? 'Hell, no'..."

"Right. Hell, no, I did not harm that wonderful woman," Jessie said. "We were a team. Like bread and butter, we were two peas in a pod. We bought Fisher's Landing together. Did you know that?"

"I didn't. But I did know that she loved it there."

"Was at home from day one."

"Then why is Hollis Jones trying to tell me Lola was selling it to him so he could build Island Vista?"

"He's offering up a lot of money."

"We both know Lola turned him down. Or was going to."

"Lola could afford to turn him down. Her house didn't have a steering wheel and a gas tank that needed refilling every third day."

"So you're selling the park?"

He shrugged, took a long drink of tea.

"Between you and Hollis Jones, I'm finding a lot of motive to get Lola out of the picture," I said.

"Let me guess: one million three hundred eighty-seven thousand dollars in motive?"

"That's an odd number."

"That's the one on the table."

"His offer or yours?"

"His. I'm smart enough not to negotiate against myself."

I took my own long drink while I pondered that thought. It was one million dollars plus the exact amount of Lola's outstanding mortgage debt. Couldn't be a coincidence. If Hollis Jones was offering the mortgage balance as part of the deal, he must not have known it was already brought current. What were Hollis and Chas up to? And for that matter, Tug? Seemed as if everyone was offering Miss Lola Carmichael a million bucks.

"You know, after all those years, she still carried my name," he said. He rubbed a spot on his finger where his wedding band might have been. "Kept the Carmichael. That's a special bond, her and me. She loved being a Carmichael."

"Yes, I heard that. Then why is your brother in jail?"

"I do not know." Jessie shifted in his seat. Took an uncomfortable sip of soda. "He always liked Lola. Now, he couldn't handle a woman like her. Damn, I barely could."

"She left you, right?"

"Guess I couldn't handle her after all," he said, returning to his almost subconscious rubbing of his imaginary wedding band. "But my family liked her. She had spunk. And Lucy loved her mama. Lola sure did raise our baby right."

He wiped his mouth, pushed his plate back. "Like I said, been a helluva week."

"How is Lucy?"

"Oh, she's doing good. Hanging in there. Missing her mama, of course, but she'll get through it."

"I meant the coma."

"Coma? What are you talking about?"

"I thought you knew," I said. "Lucy was shot on Tuesday night after the wake. She's at Island Memorial."

I hadn't finished my sentence before Jessie sprang from the booth, tossing down a twenty. "I gotta go," he said. He rushed through the restaurant, smacked into Austin Metwally, nearly knocking him down, then rushed out the front door.

I glanced at my untouched dinner, shoveled a whole chicken and waffle bite into my mouth, threw down my own twenty, scooped up my pugs, and calmly followed Jessie outside.

His Winnebago was roaring onto Marsh Grass Road when I climbed into the Mini. I dry swallowed my mouthful and nearly choked. I buckled in the booster, backed up, and nearly crashed into Austin. He was driving his mother's car, but that boy was not watching where he was going. Or at least not watching me. He, too, followed the Winnebago down Marsh Grass.

Two miles later, we all turned onto Cabana Boulevard. The Winnebago in the lead, Austin's car second, and my convertible a distant third. I kept several cars between us. I might have been low to the ground, but I could spot that camper a mile away. A literal mile.

Jessie turned into the hospital entrance, but Austin kept going. He must not have been following Jessie after all.

I continued to stay several cars behind, but kept my eyes on his car. It couldn't hurt to see where he was going.

He was going home to Fisher's Landing.

I inched my way through the entrance, watching Austin pull

into a driveway at the corner of the last lane. I braked, then reversed around an old Ford truck parked in front of Lucy's rental. It hid most of the Mini. I was pretty sure every resident was familiar with my car since I'd been there eighteen dozen times, so I didn't worry about someone calling in a suspicious person lurking in her unknown vehicle.

The trailer home Austin entered looked nicer than the ones parked down farther on flop row. I know this, having been there many times over the years investigating various petty crimes and nine hundred times searching for Jessie.

Once Austin was inside, I quickly moved the Mini down to flop row, tucking it behind a pair of campers within view of his trailer on the corner. I could see the lights on at Austin's. The sun was dipping lower in the sky, but it was still light out. The magic hour.

I swiped the contact list on my phone, dialing Sid Bassi, best friend and occasional accomplice. "You up for some surveillance?" I asked when she answered.

"Surveillance or B and E? Last time you ended up dangling from a second story window."

"And the time before that, you landed your current boyfriend and a spot in his underground poker game. I'd say you're coming out ahead."

"Agreed. I'm heading your way," she said. "Wait, where are we surveilling?"

"Fisher's Landing. I'm parked in the last row."

After she clicked off, I swiped another name on the contact list.

"Hey Ransom," I said. "How's it going?"

"It's going," he said.

"You busy right now?"

"Good timing. I'm about to call it a day. You want to grab a bite?"

"Actually, I'm calling for a favor. Can you watch the pugs?"

"Tonight?"

"Right now," I said. "If possible. I know it's last minute, but Sid just called. She wants to meet for a drink."

"A drink, huh?"

"You know, a girls' night out," I said. "I could really, really use a night without these dogs hooked to my hip. And we'll likely be late, so if you could walk them, play with them, keep them company, and not let them out of your sight, that would be amazing."

"Amazing," he said.

"Yes, amazing."

"The alarm—"

"It's too soon," I said and quickly explained how much food and where to find it before he changed his mind. "I'm headed home now, meet you there."

Five minutes later, Sid pulled in behind me. I crept out of my car and over to hers, slipping into the passenger seat. "I need to run the dogs home."

"They're here?"

"Not for long. Be right back. Watch that trailer." I pointed at Imogene's house with Austin's car out front. "Call me if something changes."

I didn't give her time to answer. I dashed to the Mini and zipped home. I spent the entire one-mile ride debating if I should actually wait for Ransom or trust the alarm system to protect the dogs for the ten minutes they'd be alone. Since I was quite possibly not meeting Sid for a drink, and he might possibly read that on my face, I decided to compromise.

I left the pugs downstairs with toys and treats, set the alarm, and then waited in the street. I tapped on my steering wheel, a mix of impatience (what if Austin left?) and anxiety (Ransom would know I was avoiding him, but was he avoiding me, too?). When his silver racer took the curve toward our houses, I hit the gas and slowed as I passed.

"Thanks, Nick," I said after his window glided down. "I appreciate it."

"Stay out of trouble," he said.

The round trip lasted less than seventeen minutes and I was once again parked behind Sid. I took a deep calming breath. Caring for those dogs was exhausting.

I slid into her passenger seat. "We should stake out in my car. It's less conspicuous."

"Mine is more comfortable."

"Mine is plenty comfortable. It's sporty."

"I'm five eleven. I don't even fit in your car."

"Don't be ridiculous," I said, probably unconvincingly. "Wait, is this new?" Her smooth white leather seats were now trimmed in black leather.

"I've had it for a month," she said.

"It looks just like your old car. I thought you loved it."

"Brand loyalty is one thing, a panoramic sunroof with magic touch technology is another." She pressed a button and the sunroof darkened as if a fresh layer of tint had been applied.

"You are my hero."

"I'm aware," she said. "Now what are we doing here?"

"I need to peek inside a trio of flop trailers in this row."

"That's B and E, not surveillance. Didn't we go over this on the phone?"

"Fine. You'll surveille and I'll peek."

"Who am I surveilling?"

"Austin Metwally, Lola's best friend's son," I said. "Give me two seconds. I need to check on him, make sure he's still in there and not wandering around freely."

I eased out of Sid's fancypants magic touch Benz. I walked around the tail end, then ducked up a patch of grass next to a cracking driveway.

Flop row resembled exactly what one might picture. Old trailer homes, some on blocks, some that used to be, haphazardly rested on wonky lots lining a dusty road. Weeds grew wild alongside bramble and sticker bushes. Most windows were covered in cloth. I was guessing sheets and towels, based on the striped and faded designs.

I cautiously snuck along the strip of dead grass behind the trailers, careful where I stepped. When I reached Imogene and Austin's house, I crept along the far side. Light flickered in a window toward the front. I heard the muffled sounds of a tv. One swift glance over the bent metal trim of the window and I saw Austin with shoes off, feet on the sofa. A bag of chips and a jar of salsa balanced on his stomach. We just left the diner and I swear he had eaten dinner. Never mind. I scurried back to Sid.

"We're clear. Austin is in the front room watching tv. Call me if he comes out to the street or you see him leave."

"Shouldn't we surveille after dark? When no one can see us?"

"Who can see us? This row is abandoned. Besides, his mother is at the diner and he's tucked away for now. I just need to take a quick peek."

Sid slunched lower in her seat and gave me a thumb's up.

I quietly opened my trunk and slipped out two things from my PI-in-training supply bag: lock picks and spray dust. These nearly abandoned flop trailers might not be up to normal personal housekeeping standards. Meaning I needed to cover my tracks. Literally.

I looked for street numbers to correspond with home lots. If they had once been there, they'd been long washed away by time and neglect. Number stickers were affixed to two mailboxes, three spots apart. Using my advanced math skills, I deduced the three trailers I wanted were the last three in the row. The lots were sequentially numbered and only ten housed homes.

I started with the farthest trailer, the one on the end. The closest car was Sid's and there weren't any lights on that I could see. Though every window was covered. The steps gave the word rickety a run for its money as I wobbled my way up to the flimsy door. I waited thirty seconds between knocks, then pulled out my pins to pick the lock.

For being a trailer, and the third trailer-type home I'd recently broken into, the lock was sophisticated. No pop lock or push lock, this one had two deadbolts. A security conscious transient surfer? Now I really wanted to know what was inside.

Though it took longer than I expected, I was not disappointed. I put the pin case in the pocket of my shorty pants and gently shut the door behind me.

The smell assailed me first. Woodsy, earthy. Slightly tangy, slightly sweet. The air felt damp and muggy. The place was moderately clean. It was definitely not abandoned. Light filtered in from an odd source: the ceiling. A half dozen makeshift skylights had been crudely inserted. A mile of duct tape plastered the corners, wide sections curling and peeling. Most of the furniture was missing. No chairs, no sofas, no bed. Instead, card tables were jammed into every corner and open space. Plastic flower pots sat in plastic buckets, the kind one bought at the dollar store. Tubes ran caddywhompus from plant to bucket. Some kind of hydroponics? Strings of LED lights were taped to the walls. Sun lamps dangled from the ceiling. I looked closely at one of the potted plants. Marijuana.

The entire trailer was filled with pots of pot.

I turned to leave and realized I had no way to relock the deadbolts on the door. Every window was covered and sealed with duct tape. After two full circuits of window inspection, I decided the window in the bathroom was the best candidate for escape. The tape had peeled nearly off. I lifted it, but kept it mostly in place, then glided the window up. Took me two shakes to wiggle out and onto the overgrown grass below. I slid the window down and inched over to the trailer next door.

Same locks, different contents. No homemade skylights or heavy humid air. Wide lengths of clothesline crisscrossed the trailer's ceiling from the front living room, across the kitchen area, and back to the bedroom where vinyl chairs and worn tables were stacked carelessly on the bed.

Marijuana plants hung from thin ropes. Some tied to the clothesline, some tied to misshapen wire hangers. The pot plants were in various stages of drying. The leaves looked brittle, fragile. Like the trailer before, nothing else was inside. No dishes, no personal items. Not a pen or a wisp of paper.

These windows were covered, but probably for only privacy. The previous trailer's windows were likely duct-taped shut for temperature control.

I stuck to my routine and slipped out the bathroom window. The street was still quiet. The speeding traffic whizzing along nearby Cabana Boulevard the loudest sound of the night. The sky had darkened while I'd been snooping. I checked my phone. No texts, no calls. The coast remained clear.

One trailer to go.

Same locks, a third set of contents: The packing room.

This space was not nearly as organized as the other two. Jars, baggies, buckets, kitchen scales, and clippers in ranging sizes littered a long folding table. I had no idea how one grew, packaged, and sold marijuana. But I had an idea that Austin Metwally was running a pot farm out of flop row.

An alternate source of funding for Austin's new golf course? Less clear was whether it had anything to do with the death of Lola Carmichael.

With one last look around, I followed my own pot farm protocol and shimmied my way out of the trailer via the bathroom window.

And right into Nick Ransom's arms.

"How's girls' night?" he asked. "Looks like you and Sid are kicking it up, a real barn burner—"

"Slow your roll," I said with my hand up. "Where are my dogs? If you left them alone, Nick Ransom, I'll—"

He clasped my hand in his. "They're with Parker at your cottage. Safe and sound. Now, let's talk about this girls' night."

"It's been interesting," I said. "Actually, unbelievably interesting. You're going to love what I found."

"Wait. I changed my mind. Do not tell me."

I leaned against the bumpy outer wall of the trailer. "Seriously. It's something you might need to know."

"Fruit of the poisoned tree."

"Funny you should mention—"

"Do not tell me one word." Ransom leaned forward, placing his hands on the trailer, one near each side of my head. "Did you purposely give Colonel Mustard a shoe to chew?"

"A tiny red rubber shoe?"

"A leather flip flop shoe."

"They're chewing my shoes?"

"I told you to stay out of trouble."

"How did you even know I was here?"

"A resident called in your car as suspicious activity. Parker took the call. She figured a blue Mini convertible at Fisher's Landing might belong to you and passed it on to me." He gently rubbed my cheek. "So here I am."

"Aren't you even a little curious why I'm here?"

"Nope."

"You should be."

"Not a word, Lisbon," he said, leaning in closer until his lips touched mine.

He kissed me with sweet lips. Soft at first, then with

growing intensity. His hands were in my hair, then they slowly dipped to my waist. One pulled me close, while the other slipped under my flowy top.

I put my hands on his arms and held on for dear life. My face felt flush. I drank in his touch, his heat. My body responding to his with tingles and urgency. His hand skimmed my bare skin, up my spine, coming around my ribcage. We were full on making out in a trailer park and I was more worried he'd discover my hidden can of dust spray than the neighbors enjoying the show.

"Hey guys," Sid said from about ten feet away.

I startled and jumped back, smacking my head on the trailer wall. "Sid."

Ransom reached over and hugged her.

"Some lookout you are," I said to Sid, discreetly working my hair back into submission. "I may have only mentioned Imogene and Austin, but you know, the police arriving goes without saying."

"I was keeping an eye on the trailer and didn't see the police roll up," Sid said.

"I parked on a different row," Ransom said.

"Clever," Sid said.

"We should go," I said and walked toward the asphalt road.

"That's why I'm here," Sid said. "Austin left."

"Headed this way?"

"No. He hopped in his car and drove out of the park."

I turned to Ransom, but he waved me off. "I get it. I'll figure it out—without your poisoned tree."

"Thanks, Ransom," I said. "See you later?"

"You can count on it."

Ransom ducked through the brush toward the other row where his car was parked, while Sid and I walked to our cars.

"Find anything nefarious?"

"A pot farm."

"Shut up," she said.

"Yep," I said. "Definitely illegal, though maybe not nefarious."

"Right here on Sea Pine Island," Sid said. "Who knew?"

"I don't know. Maybe Lola?"

"Man, there was a lot going on around here."

"Word." I paused at my driver door. "You headed home?"

"Milo's got a game tonight," she said. "You?"

"Yeah. I need to confront Chas Obermeyer, but it'll have to wait. Bitsy'll be at the lunch tomorrow, right?"

"Likely, but not Chas. Unless he's joined the Suffrage Society."

I sighed. Quite loudly. "I'll track him down. He's going to tell me what the hell is going on, one way or another."

"You get him, sister."

"I plan to."

EIGHTEEN

(Day #7: Friday Morning)

The sun rose with its usual grace, slowly lightening my bedroom. Gentle waves lapped on the sand, and faraway gulls called in the distance. An early breeze kept my room cool and salty and reminded me daily that my life's a beach.

Except today. It was Friday. The day the Ballantynes returned to Sea Pine Island. I hoped they wouldn't notice I hadn't sprung Chef Carmichael from jail or figured out who took Lola's life. Oh, and their new baby pugs were the target of unknown kidnappers.

I convinced myself I still needed to get out of bed. I tossed on sweats and took my tiny companions on a long walk down the beach, returning only when I saw the Ballantyne's private jet fly low over the ocean toward the airport less than a mile away.

"You're going to meet your new mommy today," I said to Colonel Mustard as I towel-dried his soft puppy paws. He fought me like a bulldog on a tear.

"Your old mommy," I said, then stopped. "That's not right. Your first mommy loved you very much." I switched pugs, dusting sand from Mrs. White's curly tail. "You know she'll be with you forever. Right in your hearts. She gave you the best second mommy you could ever have."

They chewed squeak toys, alternating between the red shoe and a green dinosaur, and followed me around as I dressed and packed their things. "Vivi Ballantyne is the sweetest, kindest, most gentle mommy in the world."

I stopped. "And I can't possibly put her in harm's way." I imagined Vivi in a car chase and my stomach turned sour. "You two are sticking with me."

I quickly called Tod at the Big House. "I can't meet the Ballantynes this morning."

"Are you bleeding? Perhaps a cracked skull? If not, you'd better hop in your go-cart and zoom on over here. Their Rolls is cruising up the drive as we speak."

"Tell them there's a break in the case and I'm hunting down leads," I said. Mr. Ballantyne would want details the second he unpacked their bags. "Wait, no. Tell them I was called to the Suffrage Society brunch early."

"It's only 9:17 a.m."

"I said early, Tod."

"It's the dogs, right?"

"She'll worry." I heard a car door slam through the phone.

"Fine. But you better be at that lunch early and not arrive after she does."

"Thanks, Tod." I couldn't remember the last time I'd missed greeting the Ballantynes at the Big House upon their return home. They were my family and I'd missed them. But I couldn't tell them about the kidnapping until it was safe.

The Suffrage Society Woman of the Year Seaside Brunch started promptly at eleven thirty a.m. Since Sid was their president, she'd need to finalize preparations, arriving before anyone else. I texted her and asked if I could arrive earlier. Like now.

The woman was a saint and agreed.

I next dialed Parker. I was in need of a second saint.

"Hey Parker. How are you today?"

"I have nothing new on the stolen car."

"That's not why I'm calling."

"Or the Lola Carmichael murder."

"Nope, not that either. Today wouldn't happen to be your day off, would it?"

"You want me to babysit your dogs again."

"Please, Parker. I wouldn't ask if it wasn't important. I can't possibly hand them over to Vivi this morning. It'll put her in danger. And with the Suffrage Society brunch—"

"The what society?"

"Suffrage. Women's right to vote? The island's society dates back to before the pirates landed here."

"Uh-huh."

"Vivi will be in attendance. I can't possibly take them. And I don't know who else to trust."

I could almost hear her tilt her head back, stare at the heavens, and ask "why me?"

"I'm on call today," she said.

"But not on duty," I said.

"Unless I get a call."

"So you'll do it."

"Only because I love them," she said. "Can you drop them at my house?"

"On my way," I said after I scribbled down her address.

I stuffed a bag full of treats, toys, ropes, balls, Bullies, and kibbles, and raced to Parker's house. She lived off-plantation in a bungalow four blocks from the beach.

A cacophony of barking responded when I rang her tiny doorbell. She opened the door and no less than seven dogs scurried out. Each with a squishy face and short legs. Colonel Mustard and Mrs. White were among their people.

Fifteen minutes later, I drove down Cabana Boulevard to

the Tidewater Inn. Set on six acres of enviable oceanfront real estate, the boutique hotel catered to wealthy guests who preferred casita style rooms set amongst gardens and pools to the blockier chain hotels favored by families on a budget.

The Tidewater's patio fronted a wide swath of beach, making it the perfect setting for a ladies' lunch. Tables with crisp white cloths blowing in the light breeze were adorned with flowers. Fresh cut lavender peonies, purple hydrangeas, and lilac roses in heavy crystal bowls sat center, surrounded by glass jars with white candles sitting in a sandy base.

"Sid," I said, and waved across the deck. "It looks perfect."

She was testing the microphone at a dais near the middle of the ensemble. Servers placed polished silver at each place setting, meticulously aligning the edges.

"Let's go in the green room," Sid said. "This seems to be moving swiftly and smoothly." She stopped to knock on a driftwood sculpture near a pair of glass doors attached to the hotel.

I followed her inside. It was in full view of the patio, yet the closed doors offered privacy. I threw myself on the divan amidst her open suitcase. Floral boutonnieres lined a low coffee table and a garment bag hung on a hook attached to the bathroom door.

"Lay it on me," Sid said. She sat in an overstuffed wicker chair and put her feet up on the matching ottoman.

"Vivi is home and I've not done a single thing to solve this case. Either case. The kidnapping or the murder."

"Three cases. Lucy's shooting."

"That either."

"You found a pot farm."

"There's that." I pulled my notebook from my bag and stopped. "Is that it? The pot farm? I need to start thinking suspects and motive."

"Austin killed her because of the pot farm?" Sid asked. "Where's the motive? Because Lola discovered it, threatened to send her best friend's son to jail?"

"Yeah, that might not be right," I said. "Maybe Austin had bosses. Maybe he's not a sole proprietor."

"Like the kingpin in a drug cartel?"

I thought about the three-trailer pot farm setup. It looked more like something one would cook up after watching a season of *Breaking Bad* and a dozen YouTube videos. Not a large scale drug operation run by a cartel.

"What else you got?" Sid asked.

"I found Lucy's notes and copied them into my notebook. She had a full list of suspects. Seven of them. I have none."

"None? Surely you have more than none."

"Maybe one. Austin the drug kingpin."

"Read me her list."

I explained the *Once Upon a Time* character references, identifying who was whom, or at least my guesses.

"But the Evil Queen wasn't on Lucy's list?"

"I added her to mine. I don't see having a *Once Upon a Time* list without the Evil Queen."

"Or a suspect list without Jane?"

"She's been secretly dating the man who held the knife," I said. "It's thin, but I'm struggling with Lucy's notes. I'm not sure I've identified the right people or interpreted her notations correctly. She talks about a wolf and a rocket man and something about an overture."

"Why is it so important you translate Lucy's notes?"

"Because she solved it already. It's a head start."

"It doesn't sound like it. You said Lucy shook trees. Plural. Meaning she shook more than one. She may not have known which tree yielded the killer."

I stared at Sid. "Truuuuue."

"Perhaps you need to work on your own notes."

I flipped through the pages again. "Maybe that's exactly what I need to do. And stop worrying about Rumpelstiltskin."

"Who do you think did it? Or didn't do it? Work backwards."

"Process of elimination," I said. "I think I can safely cross off Jessie, Chef, and Virginia, Lucy's grandmother."

"What makes you so sure?"

"Chef is definitely covering for Jessie, or at least he thinks he is. Jessie might be a troublemaker, but I can't believe he'd shoot his own daughter or kill her mother."

"And Virginia?"

"I don't see a thread of reasoning to connect her to Lola's death. She gains nothing, and so far, she's lost. Her eldest is in jail and her granddaughter in the hospital."

"Who does that leave?"

"Chas and/or Bitsy, Bitsy and/or Hollis Jones, Imogene and/or Austin, and Tug Jensen."

"Our Chas and Bitsy?"

"Yep. Suspects: Chas and Bitsy are building a sparkly new luxury sailing club across the street from Fisher's Landing. Motive: Either they want the park for themselves or wanted to shut it down because it decreases their property value.

"Suspect: Developer Hollis Jones is trying to buy that same park from Jessie, though first from Lola. Motive: similar to Chas and Bitsy's. He wants to develop super expensive condos on the land."

"Very valuable land," Sid added. "My sales manager at the office was just talking about how most every large parcel on the island has already been built out. Redevelopment is the next phase for growth. Fisher's Landing is also waterfront, making it that much more coveted."

"Somewhere in there Bitsy is cavorting with Hollis Jones.

He put a dazzling one-million-dollar offer on the table and Chas isn't happy. To the point where I'm pretty sure Chas paid Lola's outstanding mortgage to the tune of three hundred and eighty-seven thousand dollars so it wouldn't go into foreclosure and fall into Jones's hands."

"Sounds complicated."

"And we found a pot farm."

"That's what happens when you break into every trailer you've ever seen."

"Word."

"It's the Evil Queen," Sid said.

"You honestly think Jane killed Lola?"

"No, she's on the patio snapping at a server," Sid said with a head tilt toward the glass door.

Jane Walcott Hatting wore a white Chanel skirt suit with a silk sash draped across the front, the faded phrase *Votes For Women* printed in blocky letters, just like her grandmother wore. Literally. It looked one hundred years old and right off a mannequin at the Smithsonian, and I didn't mean a display out front. I meant the one in the way back where they kept the Ark of the Covenant.

"Do you wish it was you?" Sid asked. "To be awarded Woman of the Year?"

Jane's charity work extended beyond the Ballantyne and she was much admired on the island. Even though she'd been suspected of murder last year and one might think that would diminish one's chance at a nomination.

"Hey, it's your committee," I said. "You guys picked Jane."

"She's the—"

"No really, I don't. My role is behind the scenes—" I waited for Sid's laughter to stop before I continued. "Mostly behind the scenes. For me, it's about helping people at the Ballantyne, the board, even Jane. I don't do it for the awards or accolades. I'd like a nice thank you every now and then. Some flowers wouldn't offend me."

"Mind if I get ready? I need to change before it gets any later."

"You go ahead," I said just as Bitsy and Chas joined Jane on the deck.

I hopped off the divan and threw open the glass slider. "Chas Obermeyer!"

"I'm here to talk to Jane, not you," he said. "And I've only got one minute to do that."

"You flat out lied to me," I said. "Again. You paid Lola's outstanding balance."

"Lola Carmichael's mortgage is protected under banking law and I cannot disclose any confidential information."

"I already know, Chas," I said. "I'm not going to unknow it."

"Jane, we'll talk later," Chas said and turned around to leave.

"Wait!" I took two steps and grabbed his arm. "Why not tell me? You did a decent thing. If not for altruistic reasons."

"Altruism is one of his best qualities," Bitsy said. "I'm sure it's why Vivi and Edward invited him onto their board."

"But why not tell Lola you paid her mortgage?" I said.

"And risk she'd want a piece of our development?" Chas said. "Don't be naive. This is business. She was negotiating with Jones. If she knew how bad we needed her to keep her park, she'd start negotiating with us." He flicked a glance at Bitsy, then back to me.

"It was cheaper to pay Lola's debt than give her part of your development? Convoluted logic at best. And that doesn't exonerate you from her murder."

"We weren't even at the Irish Spring," Chas said.

"I told you, Elli, we were at the trailer," Bitsy added. She and Chas exchanged a look.

"Sure," I said. "You alibi each other. Not very solid. It would never hold up in court."

Bitsy choked when I said court. "Hollis Jones was with us. We were giving him a tour."

"Why?" I asked. "He's your competition."

"He wants us to combine developments," Bitsy said. "It's really not a terrible idea."

At that, Chas turned and stormed away. Fists clenched at his sides, marching across the deck and down the steps.

"I think it's smart to hedge our bets," Bitsy said.

"Why was your car at Tug's and not at your sales trailer last Saturday?"

"It's a Mercedes. I couldn't park it on the dirt road. They hadn't applied the gravel layer yet." Everything said in a tone that implied I was nothing more than a dim-witted hillbilly. "Oh, the guests are starting to arrive."

Virginia Carmichael, not a guest, marched straight across the deck with such force, I swear the boards moved. "Elliott Lisbon, you have some nerve coming between me and my son."

Jane stepped between us. "What the hell are you doing here?" she asked.

"You stay out of this." Virginia put her finger close to Jane's face. "And I'm talking about my family. Thomas is trying to do the right thing for once, putting his brother first, and you both are screwing it up."

"Tom didn't do this," Jane said. "You know it."

"You've been meddling in my house for far too long," Virginia said to Jane. "About time I put a stop to it."

"Ladies," I said. "Perhaps we should remain calm."

"Don't you tell me what to do," Virginia said. "You're another meddler. Stay out of this. All of this."

"I'm doing what needs to be done," I said.

"You're not doing near enough," Jane said. "Tom should've

been out of jail days ago."

"I'm working on it," I said.

"Oh, no you're not," Virginia said. "What more do I need to do to stop you?"

"Did you steal my pugs?" I asked. "Lola's pugs? Trying to extort money? Extort fear?"

"You kidnapped puppies?" Jane said. "Is there no depth to your depravity?"

"What the hell are you talking about?" Virginia said. "You mean those dogs? They don't look kidnapped to me."

Colonel Mustard and Mrs. White bounded across the deck at full speed, their leashes stretched to the limit, dragging Parker in full uniform with them.

"I got called in to patrol, Elliott," Parker said. "We're short staffed and it's been a busy day. I'm sorry, but I can't keep them."

"Vivi will be here any minute," I said.

"Vivi's back in town?" Bitsy asked. "How lovely. I must find her seating card."

"Corporal Parker, have you questioned Virginia Carmichael?" Jane said. "She may be responsible for everything. Lola, the dog kidnapping. What else? I bet there's more."

"Lucy's shooting," I added.

"How dare you," Virginia said. She stepped toward Jane, her face red, her eyes huge. "I will ruin you—"

"You're going to threaten me in front of the police?" Jane said.

"Mrs. Carmichael," Parker said. "Perhaps we should take a step back."

"This woman," Virginia said, waving her arm in front of Jane with disgust, "has the gall to say I stole two dogs? I killed Lola? For what? To run a trailer park?"

"Run her park?" I asked.

"Well someone has to," Virginia said. "Folks are moving out of there faster than a hurricane evacuation. Passed three moving trucks on my way here. No management, no tenants."

"Tug Jensen is in charge," I said.

"Not from what I saw."

"And the dogs?" I asked. "You live in Savannah. And coincidentally, the kidnapper stole a car from Savannah."

"Why would I want those monsters?"

"You're calling Vivi Ballantyne's babies monsters?" Jane said. "Have you no class?"

"These are Vivi's?" Bitsy asked.

As if following a stage cue, Vivi Ballantyne walked up the steps and onto the patio. She wore a lovely white pantsuit with black piping. Her suffrage sash fresh pressed, her wide-brimmed hat perfectly perched.

"Oh dear Heaven," I said, lowering my voice. "Pull it together and hide your crazy, ladies."

Bitsy grabbed the leashes from my hand. "Here, I'll give them to her." She tangled in the cord and landed smack on her butt while the pugs raced toward Vivi as if they knew her. They simultaneously slammed into a chair and tripped on the low hanging tablecloth.

An entire place setting of fine china and crystal glassware toppled onto the wood deck behind the flying pugs.

"Well, now, who do we have here?" Vivi Ballantyne said.

"Vivi!" I dashed over and quickly grabbed their flailing leash boxes, completely ignoring the chaos behind me. "How are you?"

Three servers rushed onto the deck. Two sprang forth and gathered up broken glass while the other reset the table. Sid helped Bitsy to her feet and steered her away from us.

"This must be Colonel Mustard and Mrs. White," Vivi said. "I am so very pleased to meet you."

They licked her delicate hands with excited tail-wagging and happy snorfling noises.

I helped Vivi stand upright, then led her to a chair. We sat at a table near the edge of the deck. The calligraphied place cards in front of us not our own.

She squeezed my hand. "Elliott, dear, I'm not a frail old lady. Edward's only being protective. I'm as strong as I've ever been. Now you tell me what's going on with our dogs. I see Corporal Parker is here. Did she find the culprit behind their abduction?"

"You know about the kidnapping?"

"Of course, dear," she said.

"I didn't want you to worry," I said. "Or be in danger. Parker doesn't know who took them."

"I'm perfectly capable—" She held her hand up before I could interrupt. "Your handsome lieutenant has already assigned private guards for me and Edward and all the Big House, I do believe. And look. There are a dozen people here."

She was right. At least a dozen women in white suits and sashes walked the path toward the entrance to the deck where a man stood. He wore black sunglasses and had a curly cord wrapped around his ear Secret Service style. He nodded once, then stood still.

Vivi patted my hand and gestured to the puppies cuddled together at her feet. Snoring. "Colonel Mustard and Mrs. White will be fine with me. You go on. You have work to do. I can see your wheels turning. You're the smartest girl I know. You'll get this done."

I leapt from my chair to kiss Vivi's cheek and squeeze her tight. "I love you," I whispered. I held her close, grateful she was in my life.

"I love you, too, dear," Vivi said. "Now, you stop worrying about me and get back to work."

She was right. My wheels were a-turning. "Let's find your seat," I said.

Sid directed us to the front table just as the staff began serving chilled Bellinis with sweet peach puree and raspberry scones with dishes of bright lemon curd.

"Would it be terrible if I snuck out?" I asked.

"I already removed your place card," Sid said.

We walked back to the green room. "Where are Virginia and Jane?"

"Virginia left with Parker," Sid said. "Not for questioning, just to calm down. Jane is probably drinking at the bar." Sid slipped her suffrage sash over her head and adjusted it. "And don't worry, I put Bitsy three tables away from Vivi."

"Thanks, Sid," I said.

"Did you figure it out?" she asked.

"No, but I'm not done."

We said goodbye and Sid went to the podium. The ocean air carried her voice across the deck behind me. "Ladies, we have work to do."

I jogged to my convertible and sped out of the lot onto Cabana Boulevard. Three things swirled in my head: The moving trucks leaving Fisher's Landing. Tug not manning the ship. And the idea he might be running it aground.

NINETEEN

(Day #7: Friday Early Afternoon)

Fisher's Landing Trailer Park and Yacht club looked the same when I parked in the entertainment slash laundry center lot near Tug Boat Slim's. But it felt different. People milled in clusters on the wood slat ramp to Tug's. They stood at the deck railing outside and peered through the picture windows inside.

The same server who verified Tug's alibi greeted me at the bar. "What can I getcha?"

"Is Tug here?" I asked.

"No, ma'am," she said. "Hasn't been in all morning." She jerked her thumb over her shoulder to the wall above the bar. The blank wall.

"Where's the marlin?" I asked.

"Good question."

I nodded toward the people by the windows. "All these people here for a missing fiberglass fish?"

"Huge fire earlier," she said, leaning on the bar. "Seemed like the entire fire department showed up. Two engines, the paramedic wagon, three patrol cars, speeding in with lights and sirens."

"There was a fire here at Tug's?"

"No, over at the trailer park. Down at the end of the last aisle."

The pot farm went up in flames? The whole island would be high for days. "Anyone hurt?"

"Nah. The trailers were vacant," she said. "Two of them burned to the frame, the other they caught in time. Though nothing left worth saving."

"If you see Tug, will you let him know I stopped by?" I said.

"Will do."

"He doesn't happen to live here at Fisher's Landing, does he?" I asked.

She laughed. "Tug? He's lived on his boat long as I've known him."

I glanced out the window to a row of unoccupied boat slips.

"Yeah, not sure when he took off. Him and his marlin were gone when I got here this morning. Haven't heard from him all day."

Some of the folks gawking out of doors began to disperse, though most of them still lingered on the deck. The sun was high and the Carolina blue sky clear. A perfect deck-drinking boat-talking day. The air smelled briny, but with a layer of sweet and smoky. It was faint. As if the ocean air pushed the heavier air away from the park.

I sat in the Mini debating options. I hated sailing and catamaraning and anything on the water. I got seasick watching the waves. Which meant I had no idea how to track Tug in his boat. Admittedly, I didn't know what I'd do if I found him.

Perhaps Tug found out about the pot farm, burned it down, and fled by sea, taking his prized marlin with him. But why?

I left the Mini where it was and walked down the dirt road. I passed the lawn-ornament crazed duo, Lola's trailer, Lucy's rental, Imogene's on the corner. Took less than three minutes to reach the end of the last row.

More clusters of people huddled together. Pointing and talking. Hands clutching, heads shaking, chins wagging. I eased close to the middle of the bunch and asked what had happened.

Same answers and shoulder shrugs as I got from the bartender at Tug's. Blaze started this morning. Fire trucks scared the bejesus out of the neighborhood. No one hurt. Nothing damaged except a bunch of junky trailers that should've been hauled away years ago.

A handful of firemen tamped down soggy charred pieces of unrecognizable materials on the edges of the trailers. Unrecognizable aside, one could see directly into two of the three pot farm trailers: the growing one and the drying one. Both were empty. No pots, no lights. Nothing. And with all that smoke, one would think the air would be heavily tinged with the scent of marijuana.

That was not the case.

"Did you happen to see moving trucks here earlier today?" I asked a nearby band of neighbors.

"Nope, nothing like that," a man said.

A woman in a bathrobe next to him slapped his arm. "Yes, we did, too," she said. "Remember that U-Haul?"

"Well, sure," he said. "But wasn't like there was a bunch of them or anything."

She turned to me with an eye roll. "A U-Haul pulled out this morning. You know, they might have been down this lane."

I was betting they were.

"Just one? Not three?"

"Just one," she said.

Slight exaggeration from Virginia.

Scoping a crowd which likely included every single resident of Fisher's Landing, I realized two residents weren't there. Imogene Metwally and her son, Austin. Funny, since Imogene rented those flops and Austin supplied them.

I hung back and dialed Ida Claire.

Turned out Imogene called in sick.

Only took me about thirty-five steps to reach the front door of Imogene's trailer. I knocked and knocked. No answer. Leaning forward from the edge of her concrete parking pad, I could see the crowded flop row to the right and straight down to my Mini parked at Tug's to the left. However, if I stepped back to her porch, I was nearly hidden from view. Imogene's awning covered the carport, her trailer did the rest.

Sid may have been joking when she said I'd broken into every trailer I'd ever met, but she wasn't quite accurate. I was standing on the steps of one I'd only peeked into.

I quickly pulled out my pin case and worked on the door. No deadbolt here. Just a simple turn lock like Lola's.

"Anyone home?" I hollered through the open door. "Imogene? Austin?"

I eased the door closed behind me and checked each room for occupants. Empty. I went to the living room. The front windows overlooked the straightaway toward Tug's, so I kept low, not wanting neighbors to notice movement and decide to pop over for a chat.

The décor was outdated, but homey. Chocolate browns and harvest golds dominated. From appliances to seat covers and tray tables to plastic canisters. The kind shaped like funky owls lined up from large to small. Plenty of food and utensils. Nothing strange stood out. Though I didn't know what I was looking for.

After the kitchen, I checked the small bath. Neat, clean, tiny. Thank goodness. I squirmed at touching other people's bathroom things.

There were two bedroom doors. Each flimsy and closed.

I checked my watch. I'd been in there six minutes already. Ten more would be pushing it. I decided to risk it. I set a timer and first hurried through Imogene's drawers, closets, shelves. Compact, not a whole lot to see. Nothing between the mattress and the flat plywood of the platform bed. And with it being platform, there was no underneath. I tapped to be sure, crawling on my belly.

One piece loosened.

Gently prying it free, I used my flashlight app to see into the dark space.

Cobwebs, dust bunnies, an old sock, and seventeen stacks of cash bundled in dirty rubber bands. Each stack about two inches thick filled with fives, tens, and twenties. Broken rubber bands were scattered about, at least fifty, all broken as if snapped off.

"Holy shit," I whispered. "Where did you come from?" Was Imogene the banker for the pot farm? Or was she the most amazing waitress who never spent her tips?

My watch timer beeped and I smacked my head on the platform. I turned it off with a swipe and gently put the money bundle on the top of the nearest stack, then replaced the platform.

I was out of time and hadn't yet looked in Austin's room. I gave myself three minutes.

I didn't even need that much. Austin Metwally had no use for drawers or shelves. Mounded clothes and discarded shoes covered the floor with abandon. I knocked through them, looking for anything odd or strange or noteworthy. Other than massive stacks of scorecards from Captain Blackbeard's, nothing stood out.

Voices drifted through the thin window and I snuck a glimpse. Neighbors returning to the trailer next door.

Tiptoeing to the living room, I waited until they went inside, then dashed through the front door, flipping the lock before it closed.

"I guess she's not home," I said as I skipped down her stairs and into her empty carport.

I casually walked the dirt path to Tug's lot and climbed into the Mini.

"Hey, Elli." The bartender from Tug's waved to me from the ramp, leaning over the rail. "Tug'll be here this afternoon. Jessie ran into him at Captain Blackbeard's, said he'd be here for the dinner shift."

"Thanks, I appreciate it," I said.

Captain Blackbeard's? The empty carport. One of the biggest clues hiding in plain sight. Imogene's car. Which Austin drove. I thought Austin wasn't at the Irish Spring. His mom helped Lola setup, then left. But mom didn't usually drive herself. Austin did. When Imogene told me about setting up, she said "we." I presumed "we" meant Imogene and Lola. What if it meant Imogene and Austin?

I flung into reverse and sped down Washburn. Captain Blackbeard's Mini Golf was located mid-island, only a mile or two down Cabana Boulevard. I wanted to call Ransom, but I didn't know what to say. "Tug Jensen is at Captain Blackbeard's. Austin Metwally keeps scorecards. Imogene Metwally stashes money under her mattress." It didn't mean anything. And the fruit of the poisoned tree just went up in flames.

Friday can be tough for a place like Blackbeard's, especially off-season. Even in glorious weather. It's the start of the weekend. Folks would rather be at the beach or the pool.

The lot was mostly empty. Except for a U-Haul in the last spot. I parked up front and went into the office hut. Dented and marred putters lined one wall next to a bucket of scratched golf balls. No one manned the desk.

"Hello?" I called.

A silver call bell sat near an antique register. I repeatedly smacked the little button on top and it dinged several times. No response.

I surveyed the golf course from the open doorway. The

plastic grass was worn. *Enter at Ye Own Risk* painted on a sign with a parrot on top was stuck in the ground. The parrot pointed to the first hole. A gigantic pirate ship jutted from the ground, its bow shabby and mottled.

Loud voices echoed from the middle of the course. Two men arguing. I couldn't make out the words. I crept closer. I ignored starting tees and the proper order of the course holes. I stepped past a cannon, then a waterfall where water no longer fell.

The voices grew louder. An oof, then a crash. It sounded like wood splintering. A man yelled. Another crash. Something breaking.

Inside an amusement park lighthouse at the third hole, Tug Jensen lay on the floor in a pile of pirate props. Blood pooled from a gash in his neck. His arms splayed out. Austin Metwally stood over him with the enormous marlin clutched in his grip. The sharp needle nose pointed at Tug's chest.

Austin turned to me. "What are you doing here? You can't be here. Get out!" The marlin remained high above his head.

I put my hands out and took two steps back. "Austin, okay. Absolutely. Whatever you want."

"Stop!" His arm lowered an inch. He was sopping in sweat. His eyes darted around the room. First left, then right, then left.

Piles of small plastic bags were spread over the floor. His marijuana supply. Scorecards mixed with the baggies.

"He ruined my system," Austin said with a kick to Tug's torso. "Tried to shut me down. I've got customers who will be here any minute. You have no idea!"

I nodded and kept my arms out. "Okay, okay. So your customers use the scorecards to mark what they want to buy? You supply it out of the lighthouse?"

He swung the marlin at me.

I flew backward into the wall. "Wait! Austin, wait!"

"Are you here to take this from me? I've worked hard." He raised his sword. "You started the fire!"

"I didn't start the fire. I swear."

He swung again. He swiped the air, missing me by inches. The marlin crashed into the wall. The razor tip snapped off. It threw Austin off balance and he dropped the marlin. It slid across the floor past me. I lunged for it.

Austin shoved me into the wall. A ship's wheel jammed into my side and I saw stars.

He grabbed a sword prop and swung at me. "You burned my entire life!"

"I started the fire," Imogene said from the doorway three feet to my left.

"Ma!" It came out in anguish. "Ma, you can't be here."

"Austin, honey, what're you doing?" Imogene said.

"I'm fixing things," he said.

"Does it look fixed?" she asked.

His wild eyes jumped from me to Tug. "It will be. First Lola. Then Lucy. Then Tug. Why won't people leave me alone?" He screamed the last part at me.

"Lola? Honey, Lola?" Imogene looked sick. Her face grimaced, her moth downturned. "Why, my sweet boy?"

"Ma, you gotta get out of here," he said.

"Lucy, too?" she whispered.

"She knew about her mom. What was I supposed to do?" He shouted and his grip on the sword tightened. His fingers were white from the strain.

"I've been looking for you since dawn," she said. "Calm down and talk to me."

"Calm down! You always say calm down!" Panic emanated in waves. "Everything's ruined. And you! Why'd you burn it all down, Ma? You trying to ruin me, too?"

"Only after you emptied everything out," Imogene said. "I

wanted to make sure there was no evidence of your operation left behind."

"You knew?" he asked.

"I've known for only a short while," she said. "You were keeping money under my bed. How could I not notice?" She glanced at me, the back at Austin. "Now, what's going on here?"

"Tug was snooping in the trailers. The motion detectors were flashing red last night when I checked my supply. He musta found my stash in the marlin."

"Your stash in the marlin," his mother repeated.

Austin looked exasperated. As if speaking to a small child who couldn't follow along. "I was meeting a buyer at the Irish Spring party. He worked at Tug's. Perfect handoff. I stuff it in the marlin, he retrieves it later. But after Lola, he quit working at Tug's. Wouldn't call me back. After I saw the alarm alert, I loaded up the U-Haul early as I could. Grabbed the marlin and brought it all here, just temporarily. But Tug seen me. Said he's gonna shut me down. I'll lose my course."

"You won't lose anything," she said.

"Now leave, Ma. Let me finish here. Go to the desk. Turn away customers. Tell them we gotta leak and we're shut down."

My turn to panic. "Imogene, don't do that."

"Don't you tell her what to do!"

Tug moved. Barely. His arm inched. His head a tiny turn.

"Okay, on second thought," I said. "Imogene, probably better if no one else was involved here. Wouldn't want a family to walk in, right?"

"Don't hurt her, Austin," Imogene said.

"I won't, Ma," he said. "You go on. Let us work this out."

She ran her hands through her hair, then rubbed her eyes. "He's my son," she said softly and left.

"I'm giving you a choice," he said. "You help me move him or you join him and I'll move you both."

"Let's move him," I said.

Tug's right eye peeked open, then closed.

"You'll have to put the sword down," I said. "I can't possibly lift him on my own."

Austin gripped the sword with both hands. "I'm not putting it down." He kicked baggies and scorecards out of the way to make a path. He stepped closer to me. "Never mind. I'll move you both."

He swung full force. I ducked. The wooden sword crashed into the wall five inches from my head. He swung again and again. Wood splinters flew. The lighthouse shook. Austin blocked the exit door.

I slipped on a pile of plastic baggies. I grabbed at the wall for balance. He lunged at me. The sword caught on a wooden floor slat and he fell hard on top of me. He pinned me. I struggled to shift him with my forearms against his shoulders.

Tug crawled forward. He pushed Austin at an angle and I twisted free. Sirens wailed. First distant, quickly closer.

"Run, Elli," Tug yelled. Blood ran down his face as he and Austin wrestled.

I seized the fallen sword. The wood heavy and rough. I couldn't lift it above my head. Dropped it, grabbed the marlin. Swung with everything I had. It crashed into Austin's head and shattered.

Austin's head dipped, but he continued to fight Tug. They flipped over. Tug beneath Austin. I dove into Austin shoulder first. He knocked over. Tug grasped the sword and struck Austin's head. It hit with a thump and Austin fell. He didn't move.

I slid to the floor. Tug kept the sword pointed at Austin.

Ransom and Parker burst into the lighthouse. Their guns were drawn, pointed at us. We threw our hands up. Mine shaking, Tug's bloody.

Ransom rushed to me. He held me close. He smoothed my hair and rubbed my back. "Are you okay?"

"Yes, yes," I said. My voice cracked. "But Tug needs an ambulance."

"Austin, too," Tug said.

Parker clicked the handset on her shoulder and requested assistance from dispatch.

Ransom helped me to my feet. My knees buckled in protest of supporting my jelly legs. I leaned into him. A minute later, we walked the chipped concrete path past the cannons and parrots and enormous jutting ship.

"I told you Chef didn't kill Lola," I said.

EPILOGUE

(Day #22: Saturday Early Afternoon)

A bright sun warmed the air to a flawless seventy-eight degrees. The salty air moved the trees, rustling the leaves of the towering magnolias on the back lawn of the Big House. Fifty children in their Saturday best ran wild searching for colorful Easter eggs hidden throughout the gardens and sporting courts.

I'd spent many an afternoon with Lucy in the weeks that followed the showdown at Captain Blackbeard's. She remained hospitalized, but wouldn't be for too much longer. I'd returned her notebook and journal and their respective Alfred Hitchcock and the Three Investigators hidey holes. Mostly we played *Scrabble* and *Clue*, though sometimes we'd talk. About Lola and Jessie and the entire miserable week she'd been in a coma.

She wouldn't divulge all the riddles in her notebook, like her star system, a secret of the trade, she called it. She said to reach out after I logged another thousand hours off my PI-in-training and then she'd share. What she did tell me: who was whom in her version of Storybrooke. I'd correctly guessed most of them.

Chas as Rumpelstiltskin, the money man. Her motive reasoning the same as mine: Chas was all about the money. Making it and spending it to solve his problems. His development would tank if Lola sold Fisher's Landing to Hollis Jones (or if he bought it for a song in a foreclosure hearing). Chas paid off the balance, thereby neutralizing the threat.

Chef as Jiminy Cricket. The son who only wanted his family's approval for paying back the debt he owed his brother. He took what he saw was the noble road and almost lost his life for it. It did boost my confidence to know I'd dismissed Jessie as Jiminy and didn't overthink that one.

Bitsy as the Queen of Hearts. One I'd given a fifty-split to. Lucy had seen Bitsy with Hollis Jones (Geppetto) and assumed an affair was lurking. She needed more time to observe them together, but she knew they were linked.

Imogene as Red Riding Hood. In Storybrooke, she worked at the diner same as on Sea Pine. Lucy had noted empty bundles (one of the first places she searched; always suspect those closest, she reminded me), and also the deleted browser history. A later more thorough search of the Imogene's computer drive revealed those online searches all related to creating a mobile pot farm, mostly from YouTube videos, likely by Austin. Score one for me for figuring that one out.

Austin as Hook. An obvious one with him working at Captain Blackbeard's. And that rocket man reference? It was the Elton John song and a line about the rocket man being high as a kite. Lucy thought his setup was pretty genius. Until she realized he might have been involved with her mother's death. That tree she shook? It was a pot plant. She stole one from his trailer and left it on his door step with her card. She thought he'd come talk to her, give her info, not try to kill her.

Grandmother Virginia as Granny. I definitely misidentified Tug. This time Lucy was being literal. She said you had to do that every now and again. Keep the snoops guessing. She hated to think her own grandmother would be involved, but Virginia was an unhappy woman tired of letting her life pass her by. And by life, she meant others getting the golden goose while she kept making egg salad. Virginia's analogy, not mine.

In the end, Lucy convinced me I needed a coded system for future investigations. No more plainly written notes jotted in a spiral left on the nightstand. She also agreed with Ransom on the security system. She insisted I needed more and told him so. It was still under consideration.

Zibby's bonnet auction raised nearly forty thousand dollars. I wore the belle of her collection: a pale pink wide-brimmed stunner adorned with foot-long feathers and silk hydrangeas. Won for me by Lieutenant Nick Ransom.

Ransom and I sat at a table near the pool overlooking the rumpus. Enjoying it, but not joining it. He poured me a fresh glass of icy lemonade.

Chef Carmichael joined us. He brought baskets of flaky croissants stuffed with a variety of delights: raspberries and clotted cream, honey ham and Gouda cheese, smoked salmon and other seafoody things I'd never eat.

"How's Lucy?" I asked Chef. "I'm surprised you're not at the hospital."

"She made me leave," he said. "But I'll go back after the brunch here. I bought her a bonnet."

"She's healing fast," Ransom said. "Only been a few weeks."

"Be out on Monday," Chef said. "I'm going to miss her when she heads to Dallas."

"Me, too."

I looked from Chef to Ransom, then back to Chef. "No hard feelings?"

"Did it to myself," Chef said.

"No kidding," I said. "Jessie wasn't even slightly involved."

"We know that now," Chef said. "Thanks to you."

"I was already on my way," Ransom said. "Less than a mile. His buyer friend from Tug's ratted him out. Scared he'd get caught up in it. You should've called me. I would've told you."

"Firstly, you would not have told me," I said. "Secondly, I do what I want. Though duly noted on calling first."

Chef stood, stuck his hand out for Ransom to shake. "I appreciate you looking into Lola's passing. Even though I didn't want you to at the time."

"What about Jessie?" I asked.

"He's heading out today," Chef said. "I'll meet him at the hospital. Spend time with him and Lucy."

"Is he selling Fisher's Landing?" I asked.

"Nope," he said. "Tug's the new manager. They're going to replace those old rental trailers. Fix it up the way Lola wanted."

I watched him walk down to the lawn, pausing by the entrance to the Zen garden. Vivi and her pug companions played with the youngest of children on the grass. Chef bent to rub their ears.

"All because of a trailer park pot farm," Ransom said.

"Who knew it'd have a security system with motion sensors? Seemed awfully sophisticated compared to the homemade skylights. I'm surprised the motion detectors weren't tin cans on string stretched across the doorway."

"He was actually a lot more resourceful than anyone assumed. A stabbing, a shooting, a dog kidnapping."

"Pugnapping."

"No one was going to stand in his way," Ransom said. "Not after he realized Lola knew about the pot farm."

"Yeah," I said. "I wish Lola would've told me that when we met. She worried about all the housing developments going on around her, but not the illegal drug trailers in her backyard. I guess she thought she could deal with it on her own."

"People always think they can handle things themselves," Ransom said with a nudge to my foot.

"Not for nothing, I kind of did."

Kendel Lynn

Kendel Lynn is a Southern California native who now parks her flip-flops in Dallas, Texas. She read her first Alfred Hitchcock and the Three Investigators at the age of seven and has loved mysteries ever since. Her debut novel, *Board Stiff*, the first Elliott Lisbon mystery, was an Agatha Award nominee for Best First Novel. Along with writing and reading, Kendel spends her time editing, designing, and figuring out ways to avoid the gym but still eat cupcakes for dinner. Catch up with her at www.kendellynn.com.

**The Elliott Lisbon Mystery Series
by Kendel Lynn**

Novels

BOARD STIFF (#1)
WHACK JOB (#2)
SWAN DIVE (#3)
POT LUCK (#4)

Novellas

SWITCH BACK
(in OTHER PEOPLE'S BAGGAGE)

Henery Press Mystery Books

And finally, before you go...
Here are a few other mysteries
you might enjoy:

FIXIN' TO DIE
Tonya Kappes

A Kenni Lowry Mystery (#1)

Kenni Lowry likes to think the zero crime rate in Cottonwood, Kentucky is due to her being sheriff, but she quickly discovers the ghost of her grandfather, the town's previous sheriff, has been scaring off any would-be criminals since she was elected. When the town's most beloved doctor is found murdered on the very same day as a jewelry store robbery, and a mysterious symbol ties the crime scenes together, Kenni must satisfy her hankerin' for justice by nabbing the culprits.

With the help of her Poppa, a lone deputy, and an annoyingly cute, too-big-for-his-britches State Reserve officer, Kenni must solve both cases and prove to the whole town, and herself, that she's worth her salt before time runs out.

Available at booksellers nationwide and online

Visit www.henerypress.com for details

THE DEEP END
Julie Mulhern

The Country Club Murders (#1)

Swimming into the lifeless body of her husband's mistress tends to ruin a woman's day, but becoming a murder suspect can ruin her whole life.

It's 1974 and Ellison Russell's life revolves around her daughter and her art. She's long since stopped caring about her cheating husband, Henry, and the women with whom he entertains himself. That is, until she becomes a suspect in Madeline Harper's death. The murder forces Ellison to confront her husband's proclivities and his crimes—kinky sex, petty cruelties and blackmail.

As the body count approaches par on the seventh hole, Ellison knows she has to catch a killer. But with an interfering mother, an adoring father, a teenage daughter, and a cadre of well-meaning friends demanding her attention, can Ellison find the killer before he finds her?

Available at booksellers nationwide and online

Visit www.henerypress.com for details

PILLOW STALK
Diane Vallere

A Madison Night Mystery (#1)

Interior Decorator Madison Night might look like a throwback to the sixties, but as business owner and landlord, she proves that independent women can have it all. But when a killer targets women dressed in her signature style—estate sale vintage to play up her resemblance to fave actress Doris Day—what makes her unique might make her dead.

The local detective connects the new crime to a twenty-year old cold case, and Madison's long-trusted contractor emerges as the leading suspect. As the body count piles up, Madison uncovers a Soviet spy, a campaign to destroy all Doris Day movies, and six minutes of film that will change her life forever.

Available at booksellers nationwide and online

Visit www.henerypress.com for details